escape
adventures of a loyalist family

escape
adventures of a loyalist family

Mary Beacock Fryer

BOARDWALK BOOKS
THE DUNDURN GROUP
TORONTO · OXFORD

Copyeditor: Barry Jowett
Design: Jennifer Scott
Printer: Friesens Corporation

Canadian Cataloguing in Publication Data

Fryer, Mary Beacock, 1929-
Escape: adventures of a Loyalist family

2nd ed.
ISBN 1-895681-17-0

1. United Empire loyalists — Juvenile fiction. I. Title.

PS8561.R93E83 2000   C813'.54   C99-932273-7   PR9199.3.F68E82 2000

1   2   3   4   5   04   03   02   01   00

Canadä

THE CANADA COUNCIL | LE CONSEIL DES ARTS
FOR THE ARTS | DU CANADA
SINCE 1957 | DEPUIS 1957

We acknowledge the support of the Canada Council for the Arts, the Ontario Arts Council and the Book Publishing Industry Development Program (BPIDP) for our publishing program.

Care has been taken to trace the ownership of copyright material used in this book. The author and the publisher welcome any information enabling them to rectify any references or credit in subsequent editions.

J. Kirk Howard, President

Printed and bound in Canada.
Printed on recycled paper.

Dundurn Press
8 Market Street
Suite 200
Toronto, Ontario, Canada
M5E 1M6

Dundurn Press
73 Lime Walk
Headington, Oxford,
England
OX3 7AD

Dundurn Press
2250 Military Road
Tonawanda, New York,
U.S.A. 14150

Table of Contents

FOREWORD

When the American Revolution ended, a new nation was born. The Thirteen Colonies, which had belonged to Britain, became the independent United States of America.

The first shots of the war were fired in 1775, and the struggle didn't end until 1783. Many of the colonists opposed independence. They remained faithful to Britain and called themselves Loyalists. The rebels, who wanted to be free of British rule, called them Tories and treated them brutally.

All through the years of the war, Loyalist refugees made their way to Canada, where many of the men enlisted in regiments called Provincial Corps of the British Army. Some of the Loyalists who remained in the colonies joined the British forces in Florida or New York. There were many bloody battles, and life in the Colonies was hard. Bands of terrorists, both Loyalist and rebel, roamed the countryside burning houses and crops, kidnapping men, and mistreating women and children.

When the war finally ended, many of the Loyalists were still in their homes. They hoped that the victorious rebels would let bygones be bygones, but the persecution continued.

More Loyalists fled their homes, taking only the few possessions they could carry with them. Caleb Seaman was a Loyalist who escaped from New York State in 1789 with his wife Martha and their eight children.

Before I could tell the story of the Seamans' journey, I had to retrace the route they followed and see that part of New York State for myself. Most of the Indian trail is now a highway, but the hills are still steep and the rivers are still hazardous with rapids and waterfalls. The dense forest is now rolling farmland, and some of the place names have changed. The Kahuago is the Black River. Fort Oswegatchie is Ogdensburg, Buell's Bay is Brockville, Coleman's

Corners has become the village of Lyn.

Escape is a personal story. The house in Rockport where Caleb and Martha Seaman spent their last days is the one in which my grandfather, Thomas Seaman, was born. Caleb and Martha were my great-great-great grandparents.

Toronto, September 1976
Mary Beacock Fryer

Chapter One

A Face from the Past

Papa and I were carefree as we strolled in the marketplace that warm Saturday morning in June of 1789. I wouldn't have traded places with anyone in the world. With seven brothers and sisters competing for his attention, I seldom had Papa to myself. Besides, it wasn't often that he had an idle moment. Our town of Schenectady was growing fast now that settlers were flocking to this part of New York, and Papa could hardly keep up with all his orders. Most days, and sometimes in the evening too, he was hard at work in his blacksmith's shop, but that sunny morning he was all mine.

Now and then we stopped to greet a neighbour or one of Papa's customers from outside the town. Near the market shed there was a crowd, and we had to make our way around little groups of people laughing and talking in the sunshine. Although it was early in the season and there wasn't much to trade, they were glad of any excuse to come to town. The winter had been long and lonely for them, and in the spring months the roads had been too muddy for travel.

As we moved away from the market shed, Papa was in the middle of one of his funny stories and I was almost doubled over with laughter, when suddenly his voice trailed off. Eyes fixed in an anxious stare, Papa was watching two well-dressed strangers coming towards us. One of them had features so much like Papa's that I stared too.

The two men stopped when we came face to face, and a heavy frown wrinkled the forehead of the one who resembled Papa. After a searching look, he muttered, "Caleb Seaman?" Even his voice was like my father's.

"Zebe!" Papa exclaimed. Then for a few moments no one spoke as the two men studied each other.

At last the man Papa called Zebe broke the silence. "I didn't expect to meet you in Schenectady,

Caleb," he said, in a tone that implied my father had no right to be there.

"We've settled here," Papa replied.

"We often wondered what had happened to you," Zebe went on, "though we did hear once that you'd fled to Canada during the Revolution, with Martha and the children. Why didn't you go?" The cold, hard words sent shivers up my spine. Zebe seemed to be threatening my father — my strong, capable father, who had always been my hero.

Zebe was elegant in breeches of broadcloth and a fine coat, with ruffles at his wrists and throat. On his feet were polished boots, which reached to his knees, and his head was covered with a tall, round hat of a type that I had never seen before. Beside him, Papa looked a little shabby in his deerskin breeches, worn homespun coat, woollen stockings, rough shoes, and that three-cornered hat he'd owned as long as I could remember.

Feeling as if the ground had caved in under me, I clutched Papa's arm and whispered, "Papa, who is this man?" Before my father could reply, Zebe's companion began to speak. Papa motioned to me to be silent.

"Zebe, I know this man." He scowled and turned to Papa. "You are a Tory and a traitor!" There was no doubt about the menace in his stern accusation. Zebe tried to interrupt, but his companion ignored him.

"You had a blacksmith's shop at Amenia during the war, didn't you?"

Papa didn't answer.

"One day, when I was passing through, you repaired my musket. Not an hour after I left your shop, I was seized and dragged into the woods by a band of Tories. How did they know where to find me?"

Papa shrugged his shoulders.

"You informed the Tory agents. I know you did," the stranger insisted. "We've a score to settle, you and I. Those Tories marched me all the way to Montreal. I'll never forget the miserable months I spent imprisoned there."

At that Papa lifted his head high and squared his shoulders. "I was a prisoner of war too," he said firmly. "I spent months in irons. You know that, Zebe. It was you who betrayed me to the rebels."

Resentment flared in the faces of the two strangers, but Papa wasn't going to be put off. "Irons that were too tight," he went on, and he raised his sleeve to reveal a thick wrist ringed with deep, white scars. I had often wondered how Papa got those scars, but he never seemed to hear my questions about them.

Papa was quiet for a moment and then he tried again. "Come, sir, the war has been over for a long time. Old grudges should be forgotten. Back in 1776

I did what I thought was right, and so did you. When the rebels took up arms against King George, you joined them. I couldn't. I just didn't believe that the colonies should be independent. Instead, I swore an oath of allegiance to my king and enlisted in a Loyalist regiment. After that it was my duty to stop the rebels in any way I could."

Once more I tried to speak, but again Papa shook his head. Would I never find out what they were talking about?

Papa went on trying to reason with the stranger. "We all have much to forgive and forget," he said. "I know I could have gone to Canada and started a new life there. Many Loyalists did. But I was born in this country and I have the right to live here." Papa's voice grew stronger. "Loyalists were promised that right when the war ended."

Nothing my father could say seemed to move the arrogant stranger. "You betrayed me to the Tories," was his only answer. "Time can't change that."

Now that his friend was openly threatening Papa, Zebe relented a little and began to take my father's part. "Captain Fonda, my cousin Caleb is right," he said. "You can't condemn him now for what he did during the Revolutionary War. In those days even families were divided, and brother sometimes fought against brother."

"You're right, Zebe," Papa said. "What really

counts is that since the war I've been loyal to the United States, and I'm bringing up my children to love this new nation."

What Papa said was true. He and Mama never talked about the war, at least not when we were around, and they never criticized the government.

Captain Fonda wouldn't be convinced. He went on arguing until finally Papa said, "We'll never agree." That seemed to end the matter for my father, and he turned to his cousin.

"Zebe, will you come home with me to visit Martha?"

Zebe hesitated, and Papa pressed him. "I know how happy she'd be to see you. She's had no news of her family for many years."

Zebe didn't answer. He wasn't going to commit himself without his companion's approval.

"Please come, Zebe." Papa was willing to plead for something that would make Mama happy. "Do you still live on Long Island?"

Zebe couldn't resist that question and he answered with pride, "Yes, I do, and it's as beautiful as ever." Then he paused again.

Finally Captain Fonda nodded to him. "Zebe, go with your cousin," he said curtly. "I'll finish my business and meet you later at the inn." He turned abruptly without looking at Papa, who politely raised his hat as the other man stamped away.

At last Papa had a moment for me. "Zebe, this is my third son, Nehemiah. We call him Ned." Drawing me closer, he added, "Ned, this is our cousin, Zebulon Seaman. He lived near Mama and me on Long Island years ago."

When I offered Cousin Zebe my hand, I was surprised to find his palm so smooth. Papa's was rough from hard work. With his vengeful crony gone, Cousin Zebe relaxed. "How do you do, young Nehemiah," he said. "So you're named after your Papa's brother who was lost at sea."

"Am I, sir?" That was the first I'd heard of Papa's brother, and I was eager to learn more.

Cousin Zebe studied me for a moment and then he asked, "How old are you, Ned?"

Drawing myself up to look as tall as I could, I answered firmly, "Twelve, sir." How I hated being so small for my age.

"He's like your mother, Caleb," Cousin Zebe said, "but there's a look of the handsome Jacksons about him too."

Mama's maiden name had been Jackson, and I knew he must be referring to her brothers. I'd heard very little about them either.

"I wonder if he'll have their way with the ladies when he's grown," Cousin Zebe added slyly.

Clearly Papa disapproved of Zebe's gossiping about Mama's family. "Let's go," he mumbled, obviously in a hurry to change the subject. "Ned, we were on our way to the cobbler's shop to pick up my boots. Will you fetch them? Remind the cobbler that he still owes me for shoeing his horse."

Reluctantly I obeyed Papa. Deep in my bones I had a feeling that something terrible was going to happen and I wanted to be with him.

Outside the cobbler's shop I met my sister Elizabeth, who was doing an errand for Mama. Elizabeth wasn't quite a year older than I was and we were kindred spirits. We told each other all our troubles, all our dreams, things we didn't want anyone else to know. I couldn't wait to hear what she'd have to say about our meeting with the two strangers.

At first she laughed at my notion that Captain Fonda might do Papa some harm, and I began to feel a little better. But just as we were leaving the shop, I saw Captain Fonda hurrying along the street with the chief constable. Behind them marched two militiamen armed with muskets. Hastily I drew Elizabeth back into the shop.

"What's the matter now?" she muttered. "You look as if you'd seen a ghost." I couldn't answer her. Were those men on their way to arrest Papa? Suddenly I knew what we must do.

"Elizabeth, run home as fast as you can," I ordered, pulling her out of the shop. "Tell Papa that Captain Fonda is with the chief constable."

"Don't be a blockhead," she exclaimed impatiently. "What has that got to do with Papa?"

"Captain Fonda is dangerous," I insisted. "I'd go myself, but I'm afraid he'd recognize me and stop me."

Whether I convinced her, or whether she just decided to humour me, Elizabeth dashed up the street, her skirts lifted high, her long legs churning. When it suited her, Elizabeth could run like a deer.

Staying well behind Captain Fonda and the militiamen, I followed them, and they were making straight for our house. With my heart pounding in my chest, I reached the house just as the four men entered it. At the same moment I saw my oldest brother, Cade, come running from the blacksmith's shop. Right on his heels I rushed into the house. Had Elizabeth been in time to warn Papa?

At first I couldn't tell. In the middle of the room stood a determined Captain Fonda glaring at Cousin Zebe, who was pleading with him to go away and leave us in peace. Elizabeth was crouching with her arms around little Stephen and Smith, who were in tears. Mama, pale but resolute, was clutching baby Robert to her. My older brother, Sam, was shouting over and over, "What's going on? What's going on?" Only four-year-old Sarah seemed undismayed by all the hubbub. Arms akimbo, a mischievous glint in her eye, she watched as though this were some exciting new game.

Through the din came muffled thuds from above. The militiamen where shifting furniture in their search for Papa. Then the sounds ceased, and the men came trudging down the narrow stairway.

"He's not up there," one of them said.

"Try the shop," Captain Fonda ordered. Cade winced, and now I knew where Papa was hidden. If only I could have slipped out to warn him, but that was impossible. All I could do was pray that they wouldn't find his hiding place.

Just as Cade and I stepped out of the door, the militiamen came from the shop, dragging Papa between them. They held him while the constable put irons on his wrists. Captain Fonda gave a grunt of satisfaction when he heard the constable say, "Caleb Seaman, you are under arrest, on the complaint of Captain Gilbert Fonda, late of General George Washington's Continental Army." Then they all set off down the road, Papa walking between the two militiamen with his head bowed.

Without thinking, I rushed after them and flung myself blindly at one of the militiamen. Cade, who was right behind me, tried to pull me away. "Don't be a fool," he shouted, but I broke away from him and pounded the militiaman on the back, dimly aware that Papa was begging me to stop.

"That cub is old enough to know better," I heard

Captain Fonda say. "Bring him along."

I was scooped up, kicking wildly. Again and again Papa urged Captain Fonda to let me go free, but he might as well have saved his breath. When I stopped struggling, the militiaman set me down and pulled me along behind him. We were going so fast that I had to run to stay on my feet.

Slowly I came to my senses. What had I done? What was going to happen to me? I looked at my father, who had always been there to help me when I needed him. Not this time though. He was in irons, and we were both on our way to prison.

Chapter Two

The Gap in the Stockade

Most of the boys in Schenectady were fascinated by the jail, and I was no different. One of our favourite pastimes was to try to picture what it was like inside. Now, to my horror, I was going to find out, and I'd have given anything not to have to.

The jail was in the old fort near the banks of the Mohawk River. The fort had been built many years earlier to protect the town from French and Indian raiders, and the stockade that surrounded it was tumble-down in places. My friends and I sometimes played nearby, looking for loose timbers and joking about the wicked people inside. What a poor joke it seemed now. How many of those prisoners had been men like my father, good men, who didn't deserve to be arrested?

All too soon we reached the gate. Captain Fonda pounded on it, and it ground slowly open. As the militiamen pushed us into the guardroom, the gate closed with a thud and my heart sank. It wasn't a dream: I was behind bleak prison walls.

Inside, the first thing I noticed was the smell. The jail reeked like a filthy stable. Papa wouldn't even have kept a horse in it. Before I could get a good look at the guardroom, the constable removed Papa's irons and pushed us through a stout wooden door into a cell. There was a small iron grating in the door, but it was too high for me to see through it. The only light in the cell came from a barred window in the wall opposite the door.

In the dimness we stumbled through straw piled deep on the floor. As my eyes grew used to the gloom, I realized that Papa and I were not alone. In one corner lay a figure huddled on a pile of dirty blankets. I could tell from his steady breathing that the poor devil, whoever he was, was asleep.

In despair, I sank to the straw. Papa sat down beside me and put his arm around my shoulders. When I lifted my head, he was smiling at me. That was Papa.

He knew when to scold and when to comfort.

"Don't be downhearted, Ned," he whispered. "We'll find a way out, but I'll need your help."

"Escape?" I breathed, hardly daring to hope. "Can we?"

"I escaped once before when I was a prisoner of war," he assured me.

That was the opening I'd been waiting for. "Papa, why were you a prisoner of war?" I asked him. "Why did Captain Fonda call you a traitor and have you arrested? What has Cousin Zebe got to with it?"

Papa smiled again. "That's more like it," he whispered, but he still didn't answer my questions. Then he must have decided that it was time for me to know something about those bygone days. He began to speak, slowly at first, but soon the whole story came pouring out.

When Papa was a young blacksmith on Long Island, he and Cousin Zebe were both courting Mama. Zebe was a rich man, very sure of himself, never dreaming that any girl would turn him down. But Mama loved Papa and wouldn't marry anyone else. Zebe never forgave Papa for winning her away from him.

For a few years after they were married, Mama and Papa were happy and comfortable. Papa had a good business and they lived in a big house, much finer than our house in Schenectady. They were even happier when my oldest brother was born. They named him Caleb after my father, but Sam, who came along about a year later, couldn't say Caleb when he was learning to talk. The closest he could come was Cade, and that name stuck.

Then the Revolutionary War broke out, and my parents' whole world crumbled. There were many colonists who wanted to be free of the rule of the British king, but as Papa had told Captain Fonda, he wasn't one of them. Eager to help the British cause, Papa secretly enlisted in a Loyalist regiment. Zebe, who was on the other side and an officer in the rebel militia, found out. Glad of a chance to pay Papa back, he reported him. Papa was arrested and taken to a prison camp at a place called Fishkill on the Hudson River.

When Papa reached that point in his story, he paused. I prodded him eagerly. "What happened to Mama and Cade and Sam?"

Papa laughed softly. "Mama was very brave. She found out where I was and followed me with the boys. They were little more than babies."

Papa's story grew more and more exciting. The dirty jail cell faded away, and I was back there with Mama and Papa and my brothers.

Mama rented rooms near the prison so that she could visit Papa. When he saw her, he vowed that he'd escape somehow so that he could take care of her and my brothers. One day his chance came. He was in a working party that was sent to cut firewood in the forest outside the prison walls. Sneaking away from the other prisoners, he hid until nightfall. Then he stole through the dark streets to Mama's rooms. They gathered up their few belongings and slipped out of Fishkill. They had to go north, though Papa knew that Long Island was in the hands of the British by now and they would be safe back at home. The trouble was that they couldn't get back. There were rebel troops all along the Hudson River.

A few days later they reached a small town called Amenia, where Papa found an abandoned blacksmith's shop. Someone told him that the Loyalists who owned it had fled to Quebec. Mama and Papa decided to settle there. Elizabeth was born in Amenia and so was I.

When Papa told me that, I couldn't help interrupting him again. "Now I am part of the story too," I said eagerly. "Go on, Papa."

In Amenia Papa tried to ignore the war, but his conscience wouldn't let him. If he believed in the Loyalist cause, he should be fighting for it. When some Loyalists working as secret agents for the British approached him about carrying messages for them, he agreed at once.

"And it is true that I told the agents where to find Captain Fonda," Papa said.

Just then the ragged bundle in the corner stirred and rolled over. A rugged man in a bush shirt and buckskin leggings rose to his feet, stared at Papa, and whispered, "Caleb Seaman!"

Papa stared back. "Truelove Butler," he said at last. "Yours is the third face from my past that has come back to haunt me today. Unlike the others, you are a welcome ghost."

The two men gripped hands while Papa introduced me. Mr. Butler sighed and said, "My past caught up with me too."

"What happened?" Papa asked.

"It's a nightmare," Mr. Butler replied. "For nine years I've been living in Canada, hardly ever thinking about my old life. Then a few months ago I received word that my father had died in Amenia and left me some money. I decided to come and collect it. I was sure I'd be safe, but I was wrong. The other day I stopped to have a meal at the inn. As luck would have it, there was a lawyer from Amenia at the same table. He knew I'd been a secret agent for the British and he slipped away and went straight to report me. Before I'd finished eating, the constable arrived to arrest me. Now no one will tell me what's going to happen. My poor wife and children in Canada don't even know where I am."

While the two men talked, I stared at the barred window, my head crammed with grisly pictures. What

was the punishment for striking a militiaman? Would
I be put in the pillory and pelted with rotten eggs?
Would I be flogged at the whipping post? Was there
an even worse fate in store for me? I just had to know.

"What's going to happen to us, Papa?" I cried.

Papa didn't reply at once, but at last he murmured
in a weary tone, "I don't know, but I'm sure no harm
will come to you. Cousin Zebe is an important man.
For your mother's sake, he'll help you."

"But what about you?" I insisted, fighting visions
of Papa with a noose around his neck, hanging from
a scaffold. Before he could answer me, I went on
firmly, "We'll just have to find a way to escape."

"Amen to that," Papa replied, but his face was grim.

Mr. Butler chuckled softly and went to the
window. Cautioning us with his finger to be silent,
he carefully removed one of the bars and held it up
for us to see. "I've freed one bar," he whispered, "and
loosened two others. We should be able to crawl
through the window, but how would we get over the
stockade without being caught?"

"We don't have to get over it," I broke in eagerly.
"I know where there are some loose timbers — at the
north end, not far from the river bank."

"Aha," Mr. Butler began, but just then there was
the sound of a key in the lock. As the cell door began
to creak, he slipped the bar back in place and went
quickly to sit in his corner.

A guard kicked the door wide and lurched into the cell, carrying a tray with three bowls on it. Papa took the tray from him, for the man was swaying so much that he could hardly stand. The guard turned and stumbled out.

"Is he drunk?" I asked.

Papa nodded, disgusted. Then he sniffed the bowls. "Porridge," he muttered, "and burnt at that." He handed Mr. Butler a bowl with a large pewter spoon in it and then gave me one. I couldn't choke the porridge down. Papa set his bowl aside too, but Mr. Butler wolfed down the unsavoury mess.

Soon he reached for my bowl and then took Papa's portion as well. "I've been here nearly a week and I'm hungry enough to eat anything," he apologized.

"We're not going to be here a week," Papa said in a determined voice.

A sound at the door put a stop to our talk. The guard entered, drunker than ever. Papa lifted the tray and placed it in the guard's unsteady hands. He even pushed the cell door shut as the lout swayed out. The tray fell with a clatter on the other side of the door, and then the key was turned. The guard still had wit enough to lock the door, but Papa, undismayed, moved away from it with a smile on his face — and in his upraised hand one of the pewter spoons.

Mr. Butler whistled softly. "It should be easy enough for a blacksmith like you to fashion that into a key. Then we won't have to struggle through the window."

Luckily no one had searched us before we were locked up. From his pocket Papa took a small knife that he always carried. In a few minutes he had scraped the handle of the spoon into a long, thin point, and he went to examine the lock.

"It's a simple lock," he whispered, "but pewter is very soft. I'll have to work carefully, tonight when all is quiet. If that guard goes on drinking, he's sure to fall asleep and then only a cannon will wake him."

Their confidence was contagious. For a short time my fears were lulled, until I was struck by the thought that escape from the jail was just the beginning. "What will we do once we're out, Papa?" I asked.

It was Mr. Butler who answered. "Caleb, the only thing you can do is come to Canada with me. You and your family won't be safe in New York after this."

"I've been thinking about that," Papa answered. "We should have gone long ago. I see now that it was senseless to think we could stay here. Sooner or later someone was bound to want revenge."

At that time of year darkness came late. The longer we waited, the more I brooded. Was it only this morning that Papa and I had strolled in the marketplace — so carefree and happy? Now, even if we managed to escape from the jail, my life was going to change in a way that I couldn't even imagine.

"It's dark," Mr. Butler whispered at last. We listened carefully. No hum of voices from the guardroom, no sound of footsteps. Papa went to the door and bent over the lock. There was a soft scraping, and then he began to edge the door open, beckoning to us to come closer to him.

Suddenly we were caught in a shaft of light from the guardroom. In an instant our brave dream of escape was shattered. We were looking right into the barrel of a musket — poised in the hands of a guard we hadn't seen before, a sober one. Papa grabbed for the firearm and struggled with the guard, shouting, "Run, Ned! "

Too bewildered to move, I stood rooted to the straw, but Mr. Butler gave me a shove. I tripped and rolled between the guard's outspread legs. Stumbling to my feet, I ran from the guardroom, making straight for the gap in the stockade. As I crawled between the loose timbers, I prayed that Papa and Mr. Butler would be able to find them.

I sped along the river bank until I reached a dark street, where I paused for a second. What should I do? Useless to wait for Papa and Mr. Butler. I didn't know which way they would come, or whether they would escape at all. There was only one clear thought in my head. Papa had said we must leave Schenectady. I had to alert Mama.

Terrified of being seized by the watch, I slunk

through the streets. The moment I reached our path, Goliath came bounding out to meet me. Before he could yelp joyfully as he usually did when one of us came home, I cuffed him hard. Poor dog. He wasn't used to that kind of treatment, but he seemed to understand that I didn't want him to bark and he followed me into the house.

Chapter Three

Stealthily by Night

I was with Mama in her bedroom, telling her about Papa's plan, when suddenly she put her hand over my mouth and whispered, "Sh. There's someone down below."

"It must be Papa," I said, pushing her fingers away.

"Pray God," Mama murmured, and she picked up the lamp and moved towards the stairway.

At the foot of the stairs stood my father and Mr. Butler. Before they could move, Mama handed me the lamp and went straight to Papa's arms. He hugged her fiercely but turned to me almost at once. "We must be away from here before our escape is discovered," he said, urging me towards the stairs. "Fetch Cade and Sam and Elizabeth."

Elizabeth woke at once when I prodded her. She got right out of bed and began to dress, but I had to shake Cade and Sam. They kept mumbling, "Ned? How did you escape? What's going on?"

"I'll tell you later," I answered. "Papa wants us downstairs right away." That was enough to get Cade moving. He reached for his clothes and gave Sam a push to hurry him up.

Downstairs we found Mama and Papa and Mr. Butler squatting around a single candle placed in the middle of the floor. Papa took the lamp from me and blew it out. Then he began to give orders.

"Martha, you and Elizabeth gather up some food and clothing — and blankets, lots of blankets. Sam, you're in charge of loading the wagon in the stableyard. Ned, feed the livestock and harness the horses. But mind, no jingling or neighing to wake our neighbours."

"I'll get the rifles and the musket first," Sam said. This was exactly the kind of excitement he liked. Without stopping to ask any questions, he dashed out of the room. Just as he reached the door, Papa warned him sharply, "Be sure to keep that dratted dog quiet."

Then he turned to Cade. "Come with me to collect my tools," he said. From force of habit, Cade moved at once when Papa spoke, but he had to know what was happening. "Papa, where are we going in the middle of the night?" he couldn't help asking.

"With Mr. Butler to Canada, to the Loyalist settlement at Johnstown. That's the only safe place for us. Hurry."

Shivering and shaking, more from fear of discovery than from the chill of the night air, we all set about our tasks. A waning moon gave us just enough light to see what we were doing. Mama and Elizabeth carried out armloads of clothes, blankets, and food — bread, potatoes, hams, turnips, and strings of dried apples. Soon there was a heap of goods piled beside the wagon. Mr. Butler appeared with a barrel of flour, which Sam helped him heave aboard. Then Mama and Elizabeth came back, each of them carrying a basket of pots and dishes and our few pieces of cutlery. Mama went to get her spinning wheel, a pretty sewing basket that was her only treasure from her mother's house, and last of all the family Bible. Sam wrapped everything in blankets and packed the bundles into the wagon.

Meanwhile I went out to the barn. There was no need to worry about our two pigs: they ran loose in the town. The chickens and the cow might wake our neighbours though, and that wouldn't do. The later our neighbours found out that we had fled, the better our chance of putting some distance between us and Captain Fonda.

I set out feed for the chickens to keep them quiet at dawn. Then I took the calf from his pen and put him in the stall with the cow. As long as the calf suckled, the cow wouldn't bawl to be milked. Every now and then I went out to the road to make sure that no one was coming.

Cade carried out the tongs, the bellows, and the hammer. Then Papa struggled from the shop with the smallest anvil. Mr. Butler urged him to pack all the iron he could. "It's hard to get in Canada," he said, "and it costs the earth."

At last Papa poked his head around the stable door and whispered to me, "We're ready for the horses, Ned."

Mr. Butler slipped past him with some rags in his hands. Together we wrapped them around the loose bits of harness to muffle any jingling. Papa looked longingly at the cow and the calf, though he knew we must leave them behind. The calf was only a few days old and would never stand the journey. "What about the foal?" Papa said aloud.

"Take him with you," Mr. Butler replied. "There aren't many horses in our Loyalist settlement."

I led the sturdy bay stallion out to the stableyard. Mr. Butler followed with the black mare. Papa was viewing the high-piled wagon with alarm, and he and Mama argued for a moment.

"Martha, that spinning wheel takes up half the wagon."

"I can't help that," Mama answered. "We have to have yarn. What about those two jugs of whisky? Why don't you leave them behind?"

"Leave them behind!" Papa answered indignantly. "We'll need them if someone falls ill." He firmly believed that whisky would cure anything. That seemed to settle the argument, and in the end nothing was removed from the wagon.

Papa sent me with my brothers and sister to fetch the four little ones. Fortunately they had slept through all the coming and going. Scooping them up carefully, blankets and all, so as not to wake them, we carried them downstairs.

As I left the house with Stephen in my arms, I turned for a last wistful look at the only home I could remember. Papa patted my arm encouragingly and pulled me towards the wagon, whispering, "Come on, Ned. No looking back."

After the children were settled, Mama and Elizabeth climbed into the wagon, but Papa didn't mount. He was going to lead the stallion by the bridle to avoid noise.

At the last moment Sam came from the barn with Goliath at his heels. He picked up the dog and tossed him on Elizabeth's lap. Goliath sprawled across her legs, tail wagging, body quivering. She stroked him and whispered in his ear to keep him from barking. Although he was so big and woolly, he thought he was a lap dog. Nothing pleased him more than to have Elizabeth cuddle him.

The rest of us fell in behind the wagon, except for Sam. He led the foal up ahead of the mare, where she could see her baby and wouldn't whinny. I kept glancing over my shoulder, half expecting Captain Fonda to loom out of the shadows and pounce on me.

"It's lucky that your house is on the south bank of the Mohawk and at the west end of Schenectady," Mr. Butler told me. "We'll be able to reach the road to Fort Hunter without having to go through the town or ford the river."

"Why are we going to Fort Hunter?" I asked.

"Because my friend Sandy Cameron lives there. He'll help us.

In a few minutes we were in open country and we picked up our pace. Sometimes in the wooded areas it was so dark that we had to grope our way. Then we would come out into cleared farmland, where we could see the Mohawk glistening in the moonlight and the well-worn towpath along the water's edge.

Much as I wanted to be big and brave, I soon began to glance yearningly at the wagon. Sam, who was just bringing the foal to the rear, noticed that I was flagging. He could never resist a chance to tease me. "You'd better ride with the other children," he said.

That was all I needed to fill me with energy. "If you can walk, so can I," I snapped, "even if you are three years older."

Mr. Butler broke into the argument. "It's nearly dawn," he said to Papa. "I think we should hide out for the day. The next time we come to a woodland close to the road, let's turn off. We can go on to Fort Hunter after dusk."

"And then what?" Papa asked. He wasn't a man to let others make decisions for him, but he realized that Mr. Butler was more familiar with this northern route.

"We'll make for Fort Stanwix and follow the Indian trail I came down. It cuts right through the Oneida lands to Fort Oswegatchie on the St. Lawrence River. Once we reach the fort, we'll be safe. A British garrison still holds it."

"Why not just stay on the military road?" Papa asked. "It goes all the way to Oswego and would be a lot easier with the wagon. The fort at Oswego is in the hands of the British too."

Mr. Butler shook his head. "That would take us too far from my farm. It's just a few miles above Oswegatchie, on the opposite shore of the St. Lawrence. Besides, I'm sure Captain Fonda will send runners along the military road when he finds out we've brought the wagon."

"You know best, Truelove," Papa answered. "We're in your hands, but we're going to have to be very careful after we leave the Camerons. Many of the settlers along the road were rebel soldiers and they're still bitter towards the Loyalists."

"Yes, I found that out to my cost," Mr. Butler replied. "I'm even beginning to have second thoughts about crossing the Indian territory with the wagon. The Oneidas were friendly to the rebels during the war."

"I don't think they'll betray us," Papa said. "They might have a few years ago, but now the new government is allowing settlers to take over their lands. The Oneidas feel threatened and they're resentful."

When the two men fell silent, I asked Papa what had happened at the prison after I ran. Papa could chuckle about it now that we were some miles from Schenectady. "Escape wasn't difficult," he said. "Mr. Butler found a good use for the window bar. He tapped the guard over the head with it and put the poor wretch to sleep."

It was easy enough to see through what Papa was doing. He was trying to cheer me up, but his trick didn't work. How long would the guard lie unconscious? How long would it be before someone came in pursuit? Fortunately Sam chose that moment to distract me. He wanted to know what the jail was like.

Mama let me talk for a while and then she said, "No more about the jail, Ned. Try to forget it and just thank God that we're all safe. We have more important things to think about now anyway."

"Amen to that," Papa said once again.

It was almost five o'clock when we reached a dense grove of pines close to the road. Papa found a trail leading through the trees, a trail just wide enough for the wagon. Beyond the trees we came upon a clearing bright with wildflowers.

"We should be safe here," Papa said. "No one passing on the road can see us."

Cade unhitched the horses and hobbled them so that they could graze without wandering away. The foal staggered to his mother and began to suckle. He was just a baby, and this journey was going to be very hard on him.

Elizabeth spread blankets on the ground and flopped down on them, but she couldn't linger there long. While Mama nursed Robert, Elizabeth went to get food from the wagon — thick slices of ham and chunks of bread. We'd have liked some hot tea, but we were afraid to light a fire. The smoke curling above the trees might give us away. We had to make do with cool water from a stream that burbled through the meadow.

All day long Elizabeth and I took turns napping and looking after the children, who had slept all night and were very lively. Goliath was frisky too, bounding around the meadow and running through the woods towards the road, until Cade caught him and tied him up.

Papa and Mr. Butler and Cade — and Sam, all puffed up with importance — took turns watching the road from behind the trees. Once I heard Papa say to Cade, "The road is busy, but most of the travellers look like settlers on their way west to new homes on the frontier."

Another time he said sharply to Mr. Butler and Sam, "Look at that man on horseback. He's a merchant from Schenectady. He used to be a rebel officer and now he's in the militia. He hates Loyalists. I wonder if he's a runner for Captain Fonda."

"He could be. We'll have to look out for him," Mr. Butler answered calmly. He took everything in his stride and made me feel that nothing could go wrong.

Late in the afternoon Mama began to prepare supper. I saw Papa take the tinderbox from the wagon and knew that this time we were going to risk a small fire. Tea at last, and not only that. Much to our delight, Mama wrapped potatoes in large leaves and roasted them in the coals.

Right after supper Papa set us stirring again. To make more room for passengers, we repacked the wagon, very carefully this time. The night before we'd been in too much of a hurry to think about saving space.

At dusk we left our shelter, some of us walking, some of us riding in the wagon, much like the band of gypsies in a book Mama had read to us. It was a long twelve miles to Fort Hunter, and I worried all the way. I was sure I could hear horses' hooves bearing down on us. Militiamen seemed to lurk behind every tree. And worst of all was the picture I kept conjuring up of Captain Fonda — standing tall and stern at the entrance to Fort Hunter, just waiting to pounce on us.

Chapter Four

The First Haven

Cade never fussed over us, but he always knew when we were miserable. Once in the night he murmured to me, "Don't worry, Ned. We'll be fine."

Papa, who was walking beside us, overheard and slipped his arm around my shoulders. "Cade's right," he said firmly. "The worst may be over. Now that we're free, we can take care of ourselves, especially with Mr. Butler to help us."

As far as Sam was concerned, action was the answer to everything, and he added his brash opinion. "Of course we can. Don't forget we have two rifles and the musket."

"Sam, you are too reckless," Papa admonished him. "Use your head." In spite of myself, I laughed. It was like old times. Back in Schenectady Papa was always having to put Sam in his place.

Then Papa took the reins for a while, and Mr. Butler joined us behind the wagon. We were comfortable with Mr. Butler; it was almost as if we had always known him. But Cade was never satisfied until he knew the why and how of things. He asked Mr. Butler where he'd met Papa. I perked up my ears and so did Sam. Mr. Butler was willing to talk about the war days, and we were eager to find out anything we could about that earlier life of Papa's.

"Let me think," Mr. Butler began slowly, going back in his mind many years. "It was just after the Battle of Freeman's Farm. That was in the autumn of 1777.

"Although I was still on my farm near Saratoga, my sympathies were all with the British. I helped them whenever I could, mostly by sheltering Loyalists on their way north to join General Burgoyne's army. Word soon got around.

"One stormy September night, a man named John Meyers arrived at my door. He'd been recruiting men for Burgoyne's army, moving in the dead of night from one known Loyalist household to another. He had to work secretly, for the rebels far outnumbered the Loyalists in that region. Meyers would have been hanged on the spot if he'd been caught.

"That night Meyers had about twenty recruits — all cold and bedraggled, longing for warmth and a place to dry out. I hid them in the barn and gave them some food but in the morning I had to tell them that they were too late to join the British army. Everyone in the district knew that it was surrounded by hordes of rebels and would soon surrender.

"At first Meyers didn't know what to do with the men, but most of them were farmers and thought they'd better go back home for the time being and gather in their harvests. When I found out that your father was a blacksmith from Amenia, I asked him to wait while I wrote a letter to my father, who lived there too."

"Why did you leave your farm and go to Canada?" I asked Mr. Butler.

"Well, I stayed there for quite a while after the British surrender at Saratoga, but I was a lot more active, carrying messages for Loyalists working as secret agents for the British. Eventually the rebels found out.

"The end came about two years later. In the dead of night a secret agent pounded on my door; he had come to warn me that the rebels were on their way to get me. There was just time to escape into the woods with my wife and children. Those dastardly rebels burned my farm to the ground — house, barn, even some newly harvested wheat and corn waiting to be ground at the mill.

"There was no haven for us in New York, so we struggled through the forest to Canada. What a journey that was. It was early October and the nights were bitter, but we made it safely to Montreal. When I had settled my family in a refugee camp near there, I enlisted in a Loyalist regiment.

"Because I knew the woods and trails so well, I was put to work as a secret agent. A few times I carried messages all the way to the British garrison in the city of New York. Once, on my way there, I spent a day in hiding in your father's loft in Schenectady."

Just then Papa decided to change places with Mr. Butler for a while. Sam, who thrived on adventure, began to pester him with questions. "Were you a secret agent too, Papa? Did you run afoul of the rebels? Is that why we moved to Schenectady?"

Surprisingly, this time Sam didn't get a set down; he got answers. I guess Papa thought it was safe to tell us now that we were on our way to Canada, and he picked up the story where Mr. Butler had left off.

Not long after the British surrender at Saratoga, Papa was shoeing his horse in the shop at Amenia one evening. Suddenly he got the feeling that someone was watching him. Turning his head quickly, he saw John Meyers lurking in the shadows. Meyers was a big, burly man, but he'd managed to creep into the shop without making a sound.

He was on a mission for the British Secret Service and needed a place to hide out for a few days so that he could shake off the rebels who were on his trail. Hiding him was a risky business, since anyone caught helping a British agent would be imprisoned at once, if not worse. Papa didn't tell Mama what he was up to. He didn't want to involve her, so that if she were questioned, she could honestly say that she knew nothing about any British agent.

From then on John Meyers hid in our stable whenever he was passing through Amenia. Papa kept his ears open for rebel plots and plans in the district and reported them to Meyers.

One night about two years later, John Meyers, who was a captain by then, sent a man to warn Papa that the rebels knew about him. He must leave Amenia at once. Captain Meyers had found an empty blacksmith's shop for him in Schenectady, more than a hundred miles away. There Papa would be unknown and could go on collecting information.

Cade seemed to come out of a dream. "I remember Amenia, Papa," he said, "and I remember our journey to Schenectady. We travelled by wagon then too. Families along the way gave us food and shelter. They must have been Loyalists, for you warned me and warned me never to talk about them."

Papa looked sadly at Cade. "You were too young to be burdened with a secret like that, much younger than Ned is now."

That brought an indignant burst from me. "I'm old enough to keep a secret."

"Then begin by lowering your voice," Papa said sternly. "If you want us to be captured, we can travel by day and paint our name on the wagon."

What a squelch, but luckily Mama chose that moment to ask Mr. Butler to stop the wagon so that she could get down and stretch her legs. She looked a little wistful and I heard her say to Papa, "When I was a girl, I thought I'd always live near my family on Long Island, but this is the third time I've had to steal away in the night, leaving most of the things I treasured behind. I haven't even a likeness of my mother. Only Elizabeth keeps her alive for me. I often see Mama in her face."

Papa drew Mama to him. "It's been hard, Martha, hard for me too." His voice was soft and he had eyes for her alone. "Surely this will be our last flight though. Take heart. Truelove says you'll like Johnstown."

Mr. Butler had more urgent matters on his mind just then. "I'm sure you'll all be happy in Johnstown, but we're a long way from there yet," he said. "First we have to get to Fort Hunter. I think we should wait until daylight. If we go rumbling through the village in the night, someone is bound to wake up and wonder what's going on. When the villagers are up and about, they won't be so suspicious of a cart on the road."

"You're right, as usual," Papa said. "And I've another idea. What about separating? If there are militiamen searching for us, they'll be on the watch for a large family."

Cade had a suggestion, Sam had a suggestion, I had a suggestion — and we all made them at once, but out of the babble came a plan. Mr. Butler would drive the wagon, taking Mama, the baby, and Stephen with him, an ordinary little family on its way west. The foal could run behind the wagon without arousing suspicion, for most of the settlers' wagons trailed foals. The rest of us would go on foot, a few at a time.

Just outside Fort Hunter we stopped again. In the early morning light, Mr. Butler drew a map on the ground to show us the landmarks we must know. The Cameron farm was about a mile south of the Mohawk on the far side of a creek that ran into the river at Fort Hunter. A bridge spanned the creek, and just beyond it a trail branched south. That bridge was the real hazard. It was the very spot for lookouts, if any had been posted. Before we came to it, we'd see a tavern on the right, and from there on we'd have to be very careful.

Since the Camerons didn't know us, Mr. Butler left first. A little while later Papa followed with Sarah and Elizabeth. Sarah had a mind of her own and only Papa's sternest voice could curb her when she was bent on mischief. Shortly afterwards Cade and Smith set out. Smith looked up to his brother; he wouldn't be any problem. Sam and I were the last to leave — and we had Goliath. Nothing suspicious about two boys and a dog, we thought.

"Are there any Indians here?" I asked Sam as we neared Fort Hunter.

"I don't think so," Sam replied. "It used to be a Mohawk village, but all the Indians fled to Canada after it was attacked by the rebels."

"Why did the rebels attack the Mohawks?" I asked. "Were they Loyalists too?"

"They were helping the British, and the rebels were determined to punish them."

The first thing we saw as we entered the village was a large stone house and beyond it several other houses, some of square timbers and some of rough logs. They were set far apart, deep among the trees. It all looked very strange to me, accustomed as I was to the wide grassy streets of Schenectady, and the tall houses standing in a row.

As we walked through the village, Sam and I smiled and talked, trying to look as though we hadn't a care in the world. By the time we passed the tavern

it was getting harder and harder to keep up the act.
Then the axe fell. Suddenly from behind us we heard
an agonized yelp. In front of the tavern door, Goliath
was locked in the grip of a huge, grey beast — more
like a wolf than a dog.

"Get out of sight," Sam ordered, pushing me
behind a tree. He ran towards the dogs. At the same
moment a man came out of the tavern and grabbed
the grey cur.

"Take your animal, boy," he shouted to Sam. "I'll
hold this one."

"Thank you, sir," I heard Sam say. Pulling Goliath
and scolding him fiercely, Sam started towards the
tree where I was hiding.

Suddenly the man shouted again. "Stop! Aren't
you Caleb Seaman's son from Schenectady?"

"No, sir." Sam stopped and turned to the man. I
was rigid with fear, but Sam stood his ground. This
time he wasn't just boasting about being brave.

Then I heard the stranger ask, "What is your
name then?"

Quick-witted Sam didn't hesitate. "John Hicks, sir."
What a good false name. It wasn't too ordinary, and yet
it was common enough to be familiar in the district.

"I must go now, sir," Sam went on calmly. "Pa
will have my hide if I'm late for chores."

Close to disaster as we were, I couldn't help
laughing to myself. What an excuse from Sam, who

was the laziest of us all and never minded how late he was for chores. In fact, the later the better as far as Sam was concerned, for then someone else might do them for him. However, Sam's reply seemed to satisfy the stranger, who went back into the tavern.

As he passed my hiding place, Sam stooped to change his grip on Goliath. From the side of his mouth he called softly, "Wait until I'm across the bridge and then follow me."

Easy for Sam to say, but it took all my courage to come out from behind the tree and cross the bridge. I caught up with Sam just as he turned south towards the Cameron farm, and I could see at once that he was a bit shaken too.

"That man was the merchant from Schenectady Papa saw on the road yesterday," he told me. "He's a runner for Captain Fonda all right."

It didn't take us long to reach the Cameron farm. Sam recognized it at once and turned into the path, pulling Goliath behind him. Mr. Butler was watching for us. Before we had time to knock, the door opened, and he yanked us inside the house. There were Mama and Papa and all my brothers and sisters.

"Papa," Sam said urgently, "we've just seen the merchant from Schenectady!"

"I know, I know," Papa answered. "He got here yesterday and has been asking about us all around the village, but we'll figure out a way to evade him."

Chapter Five

Enter
James MacGregor

"Mr. Butler, may I..."

"If you call me that once more, I'll tan your hide," Mr. Butler threatened. "Now let me hear your story again, right from the beginning. Who are you?"

"I'm James MacGregor," I began wearily. Tightening my grasp on his waist from my perch behind him, I pressed my legs against the horse's sides. "You're my father." That made me think for a moment. "Do I call you Pa?" I asked him slyly.

"Of course you do. Go on."

"You're my father, Hector MacGregor. You're a cabinetmaker and we live on the High Street in Albany. I'm your only child and my mother is dead. We're on our way to Oriskany to visit relatives."

"That's more like it." Mr. Butler was stern for a change. "See that you remember and let's have no more slips. Do you want to give us away?"

"Oh no, Pa!"

Nothing but danger on all sides. At any moment we might be seized and imprisoned. Yet laughter bubbled up inside me when I called him Pa. Most of our friends in Schenectady addressed their parents as Pa and Ma, but Mama and Papa forbade us to. They cherished the old customs from Long Island.

For the next few days I had to be on guard. Ned Seaman, with seven brothers and sisters, had given way to James MacGregor, an only child. I squirmed in the black woollen suit I wore. How it itched! I'd have given anything for the comfort of my old deerskin breeches and homespun shirt, but they weren't grand enough for the only son of a craftsman from Albany.

And how different that craftsman looked from the Truelove Butler of a few hours ago. Gone were the filthy clothes in which he'd spent a week in jail — replaced by Mr. Cameron's Sunday suit. Big and imposing astride his horse, Hector MacGregor was every inch the prosperous citizen.

About two hours had passed since our arrival at the Cameron farm, a very busy two hours. Mr. Butler's faith in Sandy Cameron had been justified. As it turned out, we were getting more help than we'd even dreamed of. Mr. Cameron was going to travel with us as far as Oriskany, where he had a cousin, John Mackenzie. He was sure that his cousin would shelter us for as long as need be.

Now we were on the road again, but anyone on the watch for a wagon drawn by a black mare and a bay stallion would search in vain. And anyone on the lookout for two men, one woman, and eight children in a wagon trailing a foal and a big, brown dog would be foiled too. We were travelling as three families, none of them named Seaman.

The plan had been carefully worked out. Mr. Butler and I would go on horseback, as Hector MacGregor and his son James. Papa would be John Warren, a widower with four children — Cade, Elizabeth, Smith, and Sarah.

Sandy Cameron would keep his surname but pretend to be his own twin brother Angus, a blacksmith from Connecticut. Mr. Cameron had told all his neighbours that his brother might soon be moving west to settle in the Mohawk valley. No one would suspect his story. Mama, the baby, Stephen, and Sam would make up Angus Cameron's family, and Goliath would go with them. Sam was the one who managed the dog best. Elizabeth was too easy on him.

Mr. Cameron left first, driving his own wagon, to which we had transferred Papa's anvil and the other tools. The wagon was drawn by our bay stallion and Mr. Cameron's sorrel mare. Papa had traded our black mare and her foal for the sorrel. It was an uneven trade, but Papa was afraid the foal would die along the way. Besides, he felt he owed Mr. Cameron something for the risk he was taking.

It was to protect Papa that Mr. Cameron was driving the stallion. Papa was an excellent horseman and one of the few men in Schenectady who kept a stallion. Everyone in the district knew Papa's big bay, and someone would surely have described him to Captain Fonda. His men were bound to be watching for a bay stallion, driven by a man answering Papa's description. No one would mistake Sandy Cameron with his thatch of carroty hair for Papa.

When Papa first tried to hitch the stallion beside the strange mare, the powerful horse reared and bucked. Papa mounted him at once and galloped him around Mr. Cameron's field several times. When Papa brought him back to the wagon, he was as gentle as a lamb.

"Sam," Papa called as Mr. Cameron set off, "if you have any more trouble with the stallion, unhitch him and ride him hard." Sam nodded and waved. He could manage the big brute almost as well as Papa could.

A little while later Mr. Butler and I departed on a horse Mr. Cameron had lent us. Papa would leave last, driving our wagon hitched to Mr. Cameron's team of geldings. Since most of the wagons on the road were drawn by geldings or mares, Papa's team wouldn't stand out.

With our new identities, the men had decided it should be safe for us to travel by day and perhaps even spend a night at an inn. Perched behind Mr. Butler, all I could think of was a deep feather bed, soft and downy, beckoning me. I was so tired that my whole body ached and I had to struggle to keep awake.

Luckily Mr. Butler was tired too. Before long he turned off the road into a patch of woods. "We'll sleep for just an hour or so," he said. In a grassy glade we dismounted, unsaddled the horse, and hobbled it. Then we rolled ourselves in the blankets we carried strapped to the saddle and were soon sound asleep.

It was a long hour. We didn't wake up until after noon, and then only because we were hungry. Hurriedly we ate the meal of bread and cheese Mrs. Cameron had packed for us and set out again. Once we were on the road, Mr. Butler began to drill me on the background of the MacGregors.

"MacGregor is a Highland Scots name," he told me. "So is Cameron. Many Highlanders have settled in the Mohawk valley. "

That reminded me of Sandy Cameron's son Duncan, whose itchy suit I wore. How gleeful he'd been when his mother gave it to me. He'd been wearing a pleated skirt of bright checks, which he called "the kilt." It was easy to see why he was glad to be rid of the beastly suit, but that skirt hadn't seemed much better to me. I could just imagine a cold wind nipping those bony knees.

We rode on and on and I thought we'd never stop, but finally just after dusk Mr. Butler asked the question I'd been longing to hear. "What would you say to sleeping in a soft bed tonight?"

"Oh yes, Pa!" was all I could answer. That morning nap had been just a tease, long since forgotten in the hours of bumping along on the horse.

Mr. Butler stopped at a farmhouse to ask whether there was an inn nearby. No inn, we were told, but Mrs. Stoneburner, who lived just a mile beyond, sometimes gave a night's lodging to weary travellers.

The Stoneburner house was big and much more imposing than most of the houses we had passed, but Mrs. Stoneburner proved to be a hospitable woman, who agreed at once to give us a bed, supper, and breakfast for two shillings. It would be sixpence extra to feed and stable the horse.

She led us into a large, warm room, which she called the kitchen. It seemed strange to me. In Schenectady Mama had done most of the cooking on the single hearth in the main room. That wasn't the only difference either. The Stoneburner house had several bedrooms on the ground floor, but the second floor was a large loft. The bedrooms in our house in Schenectady were all on the second floor, and there was an attic under the tall gables.

Different though it looked, the kitchen reminded me of home. Mr. Stoneburner was seated beside the hearth smoking his pipe, just like Papa. And the room was alive with children, cats, and dogs. In a basket near the fire was a litter of newborn pups, their eyes still closed. When I knelt to stroke them, their mother eyed me nervously.

Just as Mr. Butler and I sat down to our supper, a boy about my age came into the kitchen. He was the Stoneburners' oldest son and his name was Paul. While we ate, Paul kept to himself. After his father and Mr. Butler had gone out to the barn and his mother up to the loft to put the young children to bed, he came over to me and poked me in the ribs.

"Where's your skirt, MacGregor?" he said with a sneer.

I was indignant. "What do you mean?"

"Come on," he bullied me. "You're a Highlander. Everyone knows they wear skirts."

"They don't in Albany," I snapped. Then I remembered Duncan Cameron. "Besides, you don't even know the right name. Those skirts are called kilts."

Paul didn't like that. Threatening me with a fist, he scoffed, "I'll bet you can't fight."

"Just try me," I boasted. "I can lick my big brothers and I can lick you ..." I stopped aghast. What had I said?

"Big brothers," Paul jeered. "You haven't any. I heard your father say so. You're a liar and you're scared of me."

I was afraid, but not of Paul. Had I betrayed Mr. Butler? Then all at once Paul punched me in the stomach, and the sudden pain drove away my fear. I hit him as hard as I could, and we fell to the floor, rolling and kicking and hammering each other. The noise brought Mr. Butler to the kitchen in a hurry. He ordered us sharply to stop and pulled us apart.

"Who started the fight?" he demanded.

Paul pointed at me. "He said he could lick his big brothers and he hasn't even got any."

Mr. Butler groaned and clutched his head, while I cringed. How on earth would he get us out of this?

"James, you're at it again," he said sternly. "How many times have I told you not to make up stories?"

By now Mr. and Mrs. Stoneburner had been drawn to the kitchen and they were listening, looking very puzzled. Mr. Butler shook his head in despair. "Of course James has no brothers, but he likes to pretend. I've warned him about that habit. James, apologize to Paul, and no more fighting."

"Yes, Pa. I'm sorry, Paul," I answered meekly, much as I hated to. After all, Paul had started the fight. He should be the one to apologize. Then I remembered gloating when Papa admonished Sam to use his head. I should have taken the advice to heart too.

Mr. Butler rolled his eyes towards the ceiling, and Mrs. Stoneburner patted his arm. "It's hard for you to have to bring up that boy without a mother," she consoled.

Mr. Butler nodded and hurried from the room. Mrs. Stoneburner thought he was overcome with sadness, but I knew he was trying hard not to laugh.

Paul seemed to want to make friends now. "Is Albany a big place?" he asked me.

I didn't know anything about Albany, but that didn't stop me. "It's huge," I said. Words tumbled out, and soon Paul was convinced that Albany must be the finest city in the world.

Now that we'd made up, Paul decided to show me his most prized possession. From a cupboard he took a set of lead soldiers that had belonged to his father when he was a boy in Europe. The soldiers wore long, full-skirted coats, very different from the uniforms of our militiamen. Some of the coats were green with wide red cuffs and collars. Some were blue, trimmed with gold.

"Let's have a battle," Paul said. "I'll take the men with red cuffs and be the British army. You take the men in blue and pretend to be General Washington with his troops."

Soon we were moving our troops back and forth, booming like cannons. When Mr. Butler came back in, I was shouting, "The British are coming! The British are coming!"

When I saw him, I came back to earth with a thud, suddenly reminded that I would soon be British myself. All the fun had gone out of the game, and I was glad when Mr. Butler suggested that it was bedtime.

As soon as the bedroom door closed behind us, I told Mr. Butler how sorry I was for talking about my brothers. He chuckled. "Never mind," he said, "I slipped up too. Mr. Stoneburner showed me a sick cow and without thinking I told him what to do for her. He was very surprised that a townsman and cabinetmaker should know so much about cattle."

"What did you say?" I asked.

"That my father had been a farmer." Mr. Butler paused for a moment and then he murmured, "We're becoming a fine pair of liars, you and I."

That remark brought a twinge of conscience. "How big is Albany?" I asked remorsefully.

"Not very big," he replied, "smaller than Schenectady, I think. Why do you ask?"

"Well, Paul will be surprised if he ever visits it," I answered. Then mumbling a sleepy goodnight, I snuggled down into the feather mattress.

"Sleep well, Ned," Mr. Butler whispered.

"James," I whispered back.

"I stand corrected." Mr. Butler laughed. "James it is. Enjoy the bed. After tonight we'll have to make do with blankets on the ground. I've been counting the coins your father gave me."

Warm and comfortable though I was, I still lingered on the edge of sleep. Where were the others? Did they have soft beds for the night? I could hear rain falling, and Mama caught cold very easily.

In the midst of that last troubled thought, sleep overtook me.

Chapter Six

Foiling
the Militiamen

It was seven o'clock and a bright sunny morning. Mr. Butler and I were seated at the kitchen table, a hearty breakfast spread before us. As well as oatmeal, Mrs. Stoneburner had set out mutton chops, sausages, a dish of boiled eggs, and thick slices of cornbread. It was just such a breakfast as Mama might have offered to her hungry men.

As soon as we had finished eating, Mr. Butler said to Mrs. Stoneburner, "I'd like to pay you now." He counted out enough coins to make two shillings and sixpence. Mrs. Stoneburner wiped her hands on her apron and took them from him.

"Thank you, Mr. MacGregor." She stood lost in thought for a moment and then went on, "There are militiamen in the district searching for two men who are wanted in Schenectady."

"Are there?" Mr. Butler's voice was steady.

"Yes, they came to our door yesterday."

"Why are the men wanted?" Mr. Butler asked.

"The militiamen didn't tell us. All they said was that there are two of them, one named Seaman and the other Butler." She peered at us for a moment, her eyes puzzled. Then in a gentle tone she said, "Take care on your journey. I wish you Godspeed." One thing was clear. Mrs. Stoneburner might suspect that we weren't really the MacGregors, but we had nothing to fear from her.

"Thank you, Mrs. Stoneburner. We'll take care." Mr. Butler looked pleased with himself. And why not? He'd found out what he wanted to know without having to probe. Now we had been warned. We certainly would take care, great care, to avoid Captain Fonda's men.

"We must be on our way, James," he said to me. "Do you want to say good-bye to Paul while I saddle the horse?" But the last thing I wanted was to leave him just then, and I followed him out to the stableyard.

While he brushed down the horse, Mr. Butler tried to reassure me. He seemed to know the dreadful thoughts that were running through my head. "There are many settlers travelling west," he said "The militiamen can't possibly question all of them. Even if they stop your father, they'll have no reason to suspect John Warren with his four motherless children."

The more he talked, the better I felt, and soon I stooped to watch him check the horse's feet. Scraping away the dung and the straw, he probed the soft frog of the hoof for hidden stones that might lame the horse. Then I helped him with the saddle and tightened the straps that held our rolled blankets. We were ready to leave.

Mr. and Mrs. Stoneburner were in the stableyard to bid us farewell, but Paul was nowhere to be seen. When we reached the end of the lane, we found him waiting for us. He waved and came running to the horse's side.

"Will you be stopping here on your way back?" he asked eagerly. We had to say yes in case the militiamen returned to question the Stoneburners.

A few hours later we reached a little town called Canajoharie. Bright and peaceful in the morning sunshine, its narrow streets and scattered houses reminded me of Fort Hunter. "It doesn't look much like Schenectady, does it?" I said to Mr. Butler.

"That's because Schenectady was built much

earlier," he told me. "In those days the Dutch settlers copied the tall, narrow houses and wide, grassy streets of Albany."

On and on we went, spending the next two nights in the woods, resting but not really sleeping. After that first morning, a chilling rain fell steadily. Our clothes and blankets were always damp, and the cold seemed to settle in our bones. Every time we passed an inn, I pointed it out to Mr. Butler, though I knew we needed our few remaining coins for food. By day I studied the wagons on the road, half hoping to catch a glimpse of Mama or Papa, half hoping that I wouldn't. Much as I longed to see them, I wanted them to be safe ahead of us.

Once we did stop at an inn — for a meal. At the table with us were some travellers who told the innkeeper quite openly that they were Loyalists on their way to Canada. I couldn't understand that until later Mr. Butler explained that they had nothing to fear. The settlers in the Mohawk valley were glad to be rid of them.

"Then why can't we tell people we're Loyalists on our way to Canada?" I asked him.

"You know our case is different," he replied. "Your father and I are wanted men. Captain Fonda may even have offered a reward for our capture."

Then into those endless, dismal hours fell one bright ray of light. While we were chatting about

Johnstown, Mr. Butler told me that the closest school was more than sixty miles away at a place called Kingston, and the fees were high. Even if Papa decided to settle near Kingston, it would be years before he could afford to send me to school. That suited me very well.

When Papa first came to Schenectady, he had very little money. Mama had to teach Cade and Sam at home. She was well educated, better than Papa, though he could read and write. Many of our neighbours in Schenectady couldn't even do that.

Then when I was six, Mama began to give Elizabeth and me lessons. There was a school for girls, but Mama couldn't spare Elizabeth for the whole day. She needed her at home to help with the little ones.

Those lessons ended for me when I was ten and Papa sent me to the grammar school, impressing on me that I was a very lucky boy. With some schooling I might be apprenticed to a surveyor or a lawyer. He bitterly regretted that he hadn't been able to do as much for Cade and Sam, but he was training them to be blacksmiths.

Everyone told me how lucky I was, but no one warned me about the long hours when I would hardly dare to stir for fear of punishment, nor about the floggings that drew blood. Mama was always fair, even as a teacher, but the masters at the school were bullies, and the big boys followed their example.

Small as I was, I was a perfect target for them. Over and over I begged to be allowed to stay at home, but Papa was determined that I would go to school and get an education, which I would appreciate when I was older. Well, that was Papa's view. All I knew was that school certainly wasn't one of the things I might miss in Canada.

"Did you like school?" I asked Mr. Butler.

"I didn't go to school until I was sixteen," he answered, "and then only for a few months in the winter."

"But you can read and write," I said.

"I could read and write before I went to school," he answered. "My father taught me and my brothers."

On the fifth day of our journey, we entered a deep gorge, which Mr. Butler told me had been the site of the Battle of Oriskany.

"Tell me about it," I urged.

"It was a bloody battle," he said. "I heard about it from a man who survived it. From the top of this gorge, a band of Loyalists and Indians opened fire on a column of rebel soldiers marching to Fort Stanwix. Then they charged the rebels and fought fiercely hand to hand. By the end of the day hundreds of men from both sides lay dead or wounded in the gorge."

To Mr. Butler it was all still very vivid, but to me it seemed no more real than the game of lead soldiers I'd played with Paul Stoneburner.

We were getting close to Oriskany, the last village on the western frontier, beyond which lay the lands of the Oneidas. Just outside the village we saw a line of wagons drawn up. Mr. Butler spoke to the driver of the last wagon in the line, a rough-looking man. "Can you tell us what's delaying the wagons?"

"Militiamen are searching for two wanted men," he answered gruffly. "I had hoped to be miles beyond Oriskany before nightfall, but not if this goes on much longer."

"That's a pity, sir." Mr. Butler's manner matched his fine clothes. "I hope we'll be allowed to pass."

The driver shrugged. We were no concern of his.

"We'll ride boldly past the militiamen and pray that they don't stop us," Mr. Butler muttered to me.

I was dumb with fear. All along I'd known that we might come face to face with militiamen searching for us, but now the moment had really arrived.

When we reached the first wagon in the line, Mr. Butler, cool as you please, slowed the horse and looked around, curious but apparently unconcerned. That first wagon drew my eyes like a magnet. It belonged to a large family, not unlike my own. The wagon had been torn apart, and their belongings were strewn all over the road. Knowing that we were the cause of their rough treatment made me feel very guilty.

The militiamen noticed us and one called out

sternly, "Halt!" Mr. Butler calmly brought the horse to a stop.

"Your name, sir!" It was an order not a question.

"Hector MacGregor and my son James."

"From what place, sir?"

"Albany."

"Where are you bound, sir?" The militiaman's tone was softer now.

"Oriskany, to look for land." Mr. Butler's answer puzzled me until I realized that we were too close to Oriskany to say that we were on our way to visit relatives. The militiamen would ask who they were. What could Mr. Butler tell them without endangering the Mackenzies?

"You have no wagon," the militiaman said, "no furniture, no baggage."

I held my breath. How would Mr. Butler explain that?

"We haven't come to settle now," he said. "If I find suitable land, I'll go back to Albany and put my affairs in order there. Then I'll bring my belongings up the Mohawk by boat."

"You may proceed, sir." The militiamen stepped out of the way. Mr. Butler nodded politely and pressed the horse forward.

After passing through the village, we soon reached the open road. Mr. Cameron had told us that the Mackenzie farm lay a mile west of Oriskany.

We weren't far from our goal when right out of the blue I had a terrifying thought.

"Pa," I gasped, "which wagon is the family Bible in?"

Mr. Butler pulled the horse up sharply and turned to look at me. "Your own, I think. Why?"

I gazed at him in horror. "All our names and the dates of our births are written clearly on the first page. What if Papa is still behind us? Will he see the line of wagons in time? Will he realize they're being searched? Will he remember the Bible?"

"Calmly now," Mr. Butler answered. "Your father may have passed Oriskany before the search began. If he hasn't reached Oriskany yet, we'll be in time to warn him."

"How?" I was frantic. "If we go back along the road, the militiamen will become suspicious."

Mr. Butler dismounted and beckoned to me. When I was on the ground, he led the horse into a field, which sloped down to the bank of the Mohawk. "The towpath," he said, pointing to the narrow beaten path along the water's edge.

"What a blockhead I am," I exclaimed, wondering why I hadn't thought of it myself. The towpath in Schenectady was a favourite haunt of mine, and I knew it followed the Mohawk a long way. When the wind wasn't strong enough to propel the boats, horses were sometimes used to pull them upstream.

The thought of Papa in such danger drove all fears for myself right out of my head, and I began to scheme. I'd walk back along the towpath, skirting the village. Even if the militiamen saw me, they'd never recognize me at that distance. Once past the line of wagons, I'd climb back to the road, find a hiding place, and wait for Papa.

"I'll go back to warn Papa," I said eagerly.

Mr. Butler hesitated. "No, I'd better go. You take the horse on to the Mackenzie farm."

"Please let me go," I pleaded. "You're the one the militiamen are looking for. Remember Mrs. Stoneburner said they told her two men — not two men and a boy."

He thought for a moment. "You're right, but ..."

I didn't let him finish. As I ran towards the towpath, he called, "Where will you wait for your father? I must know where to find you if he's already at the Mackenzies'."

Without stopping, I called back, "There was a milestone on the road, just before we reached the line of wagons. I'll hide in the bushes behind it."

"Very well then," Mr. Butler answered. "Godspeed, Ned."

When I reached the towpath, I turned eastward. There was one bad moment just outside the village. I saw a small group of people walking towards me, but all they did was greet me politely and go on their way.

Once I was sure I was east of the line of wagons, I climbed back to the road. The first thing I had to do was find out whether Papa's wagon had joined the line. Keeping close to the bushes, I walked back a short distance along the road.

There were just two wagons in the line now, the second one that of the surly man we'd talked to earlier. Papa hadn't arrived yet. I sped back to the milestone and crawled into a clump of bushes. From my hiding place I could see the road, but no one could see me.

The woods grew shadowy, though the sun still shone on the road beyond the trees. Oddly enough, I wasn't frightened now. My only thought was to warn Papa in time.

Chapter Seven

Farewell, James MacGregor

Suddenly the quiet of my cramped hiding place was shattered by the snapping of a twig. Then I heard a high-pitched yelp — and a furry body crashed into the bushes on top of me. Not a wolf, not a bear, but Goliath, and from above came Sam's unmistakable voice.

"Ned! What in the world ... where is Mr. Butler?"

"Where's Mama?" I demanded, picking myself up and climbing out of the bushes. "Why are you here?"

Goliath danced in a circle around us, barking

shrilly, leaping first at Sam and then at me. Sam grabbed him and cuffed him hard. "Enough of that hullabaloo," he said sternly. Goliath looked at him reproachfully, then put his paws on my shoulders and set to licking my face.

Sam shook his head in disgust and answered me. "I'm here for the same reason as you, I guess. Did Mr. Butler send you to warn Papa that the militiamen are searching the wagons?"

I nodded, a little disappointed that I wasn't the hero of the day after all. The others had remembered the Bible too.

"Where's Mama?" I repeated.

"Safe at the Mackenzie cabin by now. We got past the militiamen without a hitch. They didn't even question Mr. Cameron's story. Once we were out of sight of the search party, Mr. Cameron sent me back along the towpath to warn Papa."

"At least Mama is safe," I breathed. "All we have to do is warn Papa."

"Warn Papa," Sam scoffed. "Papa must be halfway along the towpath by now. I stopped our wagon about a mile back and persuaded him to go the rest of the way on foot. He didn't want to leave Cade and Elizabeth and the children but he finally had to admit that they'd be safer without him. I was going to wait here in the bushes to give him time to clear the village. If Goliath hadn't scented you, you'd never have known I was here."

"What did you do with the Bible?" I asked.

"It's still in the wagon. What about it?"

"Our names are written in it, you blockhead."

Sam's smug look disappeared quickly. "All we thought about was getting Papa out of the wagon in time. He didn't remember the Bible either."

"We have to warn Cade," I broke in, running out to the road. Sam and Goliath were close behind me. Before we'd gone a quarter of a mile, we saw our wagon approaching us. That dratted Goliath set up a din as soon as it stopped, and he wouldn't let up until Sam boosted him into the wagon beside Elizabeth.

"Ned, what in the world ...?" Cade exclaimed, in the very words Sam had used when Goliath pounced on me in the bushes.

"We have to get rid of the Bible," I gasped.

"Why?" Cade asked.

"Because of our names."

Without a word, Elizabeth began to rummage in the back of the wagon. Almost at once she turned with the Bible in her outstretched hands, holding it very gingerly as though afraid it might burn her.

"What shall we do with it?" she asked.

"Throw it away," Sam advised in his hasty way.

"No," Cade disagreed, "it means too much to Mama. Besides, it contains the only proof of our ages."

"I've got another idea then," Sam said. "I'll wrap

it in a blanket with some clothes and carry it on my back. If anyone questions me, I'll say that I'm an orphan looking for a place to apprentice. I don't think anyone will bother to search my pack. Ned can go with you. He looks too tired to walk all the way to the Mackenzie farm."

"That's a stupid idea," I retorted, stung by his superior tone. "The militiamen have already had a good look at me on the back of Mr. Butler's horse."

"Then come with me," he said unabashed. "We'll be two orphan brothers looking for work."

"With you in those tattered breeches and shirt and me in this suit," I snapped. Although I'd slept in the suit for several nights, it still looked a lot better than Sam's clothes. "We don't look much like brothers. I'll go alone."

"You'll go with Sam along the towpath," Cade said firmly. "Elizabeth, find Ned's clothes."

I started to protest, but Cade cut me off. "Let's have no more argument," he said, in voice so much like Papa's that I hastened to obey.

As soon as I stepped out of the itchy black suit, I began to feel better. Even with Cade treating me as though I were no older than Smith, I was glad to be Ned Seaman again. And no matter how much Sam lorded it over me, I was the only one who had remembered the Bible.

By the time I'd finished changing my clothes, Sam

had the pack on his back and was urging me to hurry. As I came from behind the wagon still tucking in my shirt, Sarah reached over the side and almost tumbled to the road. "Me too," she giggled, stretching out her arms. Elizabeth pulled her back and shushed her as Sam and I sped away towards the towpath.

"Do you think the militiamen will stop Cade?" I asked Sam.

"What if they do?" he answered. "Cade will make up a good story to tell them, or Elizabeth will. The only thing that could have given them away was the Bible, and we have that."

As far as Sam was concerned, the matter was settled, and he wanted to find out what had happened to Mr. Butler and me on our journey from Fort Hunter. Since he was hardly ever interested in anything I had to say, I made the most of this chance. Intent on telling him about our adventures, I didn't even notice the two militiamen on the towpath until we were almost up to them.

"It's too late to turn back now," Sam murmured. "Keep walking and don't be timid."

That was easy for Sam to say, but it was all I could do not to take to my heels. Maybe they won't pay any attention to us, I tried to tell myself, but no such luck. They ordered us to halt and demanded to know our names.

Fear had robbed me of speech, but Sam's reply

came as quick as a flash. "John Hicks, sir, and my brother Joseph." The false name he'd given the merchant at the tavern — and then he went right into his story about two orphans looking for work.

"Orphans you may be," one of the militiamen retorted sharply, "but I wonder if you are thieves as well. Hand me your pack."

"I'm an honest lad," Sam protested, undaunted. "There's nothing in my pack that doesn't belong to me."

Before Sam could get the pack off his back, one of the militiamen seized him and began to tug at it — so hard that Sam winced. Then the two men put the pack on the ground and spread open the blanket.

"Nothing here except their clothes and this Bible," one of them said. Holding the book by the spine, he shook it hard as though expecting something important to fall out from between the pages. Then without a word he dropped the Bible on the pile of clothes. I couldn't believe it. He'd looked right at the page where Papa had written all our names.

"You may go on," we were told, and Sam stooped to roll up his pack.

"Come along, Joseph," he said to me sharply.

As soon as we were out of earshot of the militiamen, the questions I'd been holding back exploded. "Didn't they see our names? Why did they let us go?"

"They saw our names all right," Sam answered, still a little tense.

"Why didn't they arrest us then?" I asked, bewildered. "Do you think they've stopped searching for the Seamans?"

"Of course not. They're still looking for the Seamans." Sam was teasing me now.

Suddenly the light dawned. "They can't read," I exclaimed.

Sam laughed. "It took you long enough to figure that out, and you're the one who's been to school."

Now that the danger was past, I could laugh about it too, but soon I began to fret again. How long would Cade be held up? It was already dusk. He'd never find his way to the Mackenzie farm in the dark.

Once clear of the village, we turned off the towpath and climbed back to the road. Mr. Cameron had told us that there were three or four other cabins near the Mackenzies'. We'd recognize it by the two tall oaks that stood like sentinels on either side of the lane that led from the road to the cabin, which was set well back among the trees. The Mackenzies had been there for less than a year and hadn't been able to clear much of their land yet.

Just as we passed between the two oaks, we heard the rumble of wagon wheels and scrambled out of sight, but not for long. It was our own wagon. Cade pulled the horses to a stop when he saw us.

"I told the militiamen that we were on our way to join our father who is a fur trader out west, and they let us pass," he called in triumph. "We're safe. That was a good day's work, Ned. It would have been a different story if they'd seen the Bible."

Much he knows, I thought to myself, as Sam and I climbed into the wagon. Then we all turned to statues as a form stepped out from behind a tree, but it was only Mr. Butler.

"Drive right down behind the cabin," he said to Cade as Sam pulled him into the wagon.

"Did Papa get here safely?" I asked, almost afraid to hear the answer.

"We all got here safely," he replied quickly, putting his arm around my shoulders.

Moments later the wagon was drawn up in a grove of trees behind the cabin, right beside Mr. Cameron's. "Go in through the back window," Mr. Butler told us, "just in case there's someone watching."

As I waited my turn, I murmured, "Farewell, James MacGregor."

"And farewell to your Pa," Mr. Butler chuckled as he boosted me up to the window.

Chapter Eight

Plots and Shots

"Thank God you're all safe," I heard Papa whisper as he scooped up Sarah and Smith, who were just ahead of me.

As I scrambled over the windowsill, I was conscious of eyes peering at me from every corner of the room. Dimly lit by candles, the cabin was like a crowded cave. The door was closed, the curtains were drawn, and a breathless hush hung over the room.

For a moment I stood bewildered. Then the cabin came to life. There seemed to me to be dozens

of children, and I wasn't far wrong. It turned out that
the Mackenzies had eight too. In the gloom one face
was clear to me — Mama's — and I went to her
quickly and hugged her hard. When I lifted my head,
I saw that Sam had found a place on the floor, with
his back against the wall.

I had hardly settled myself beside him when Morag
Mackenzie, a girl not much older than Elizabeth,
turned from the hearth with a bowl of stew in each
hand. There was a lively gleam in Sam's eye as he took
one from her. Mr. Butler, who was easing himself to
the floor beside us, looked at Sam and Morag and then
he winked at me — but he didn't say anything.

Our encounter with the two militiamen on the
towpath was still very much on my mind, and I began
to tell Mr. Butler about it. "Just imagine," I concluded,
"Sam and I were saved because they couldn't read. Papa
would say that proves what he often tells us about the
advantages of a good education."

Mr. Butler laughed as he moved to make room for
Papa, who was already intent on plans for the next
step of our journey. "What now, Truelove?" he asked.

"Well," Mr. Butler answered, "we're about six
miles from Fort Stanwix and the Indian trail to
Oswegatchie. I'm convinced that's the route we
should take. The tricky thing is to reach the trail
without being seen. We want Captain Fonda to
think we've taken the road to Oswego."

"Easier said than done," Papa mused.

"You're right, Caleb. It's going to be risky, but travelling in small groups has worked pretty well up to now. I think we should try it again." Mr. Butler looked at Mr. Cameron as though seeking his help.

Mr. Cameron shook his head. "I'm very sorry but I have to get back to Fort Hunter to keep an appointment."

"Don't apologize," Papa interrupted hastily. "You've done more than enough already, and I'm more grateful than I can tell you."

Sam and Cade had been whispering, their heads close together, and now Cade spoke up. "Papa, I think you and Mr. Butler should make your way on foot through the forest to the Indian trail. We'll be safer without you on the road. If we're questioned, I'll say that we're on our way to Lake Oneida to join our father, who is a fur trader. That story worked before."

"I just don't know what would be the wisest thing to do," Papa murmured.

"It's only six miles," Cade insisted. "Let's do it my way and meet on the trail." It wasn't like Cade to argue with Papa. There was something in the wind. That's what the whispering had been all about. Sam had hatched some daring plan and had persuaded Cade to go along with it.

"Cade's right," Mr. Butler said. "We'd better go through the forest, Caleb, and take Ned with us.

We're the ones who might be recognized by searchers on the road."

Much as I wanted to fall in with their plans, I just couldn't. I was too bone weary. "I'd rather go in the wagon," I said sheepishly. "What about a disguise? I could loosen my hair and wear one of Elizabeth's dresses."

"As long as you remember to keep your big feet hidden," Sam taunted, but at least he didn't tease me about being too puny to walk through the forest.

Papa was silent for a while and then he said almost to himself, "There doesn't seem to be any other way. If we didn't need the wagon to carry our provisions, we could all walk through the woods."

It was clear that Mr. Butler didn't want Papa to ponder any longer. "You're right, Caleb," he said firmly. "We must take the wagon as far as we can, even if we have to abandon it when we reach the Long Falls. The trail gets pretty rugged from there on, but we'll see."

"I hope I'm doing the right thing," Papa said. "If the worst comes to the worst, and my wife and children are captured, the militiamen are bound to release them if I surrender."

"Over my dead body," Sam whispered to Cade and me.

"Listen carefully, all of you," Mr. Butler said. "The Indian trail branches off the road just south of

Fort Stanwix. Be on the lookout for it as soon as you catch sight of the fort."

"Are there soldiers at the fort?" I asked, rather worried.

"No," Mr. Butler replied. "It's been empty since the war ended, and there aren't any settlers nearby either. The land is too swampy."

"Where shall we meet?" Cade asked.

"There's a small camp the Oneidas use when they're hunting, about two miles along the trail. There are no longhouses, only a few small bark shelters. We'll meet there," Mr. Butler replied.

While we'd been talking, Mama and Mrs. Mackenzie had been sorting out blankets and trying to find places for all of us to sleep, and it wasn't an easy task with so many of us. Finally they decided that all the men and boys would go to the loft, while the women and girls settled down in the main room of the cabin.

Papa called us before dawn. By lamplight he and Mr. Butler removed the anvil and the other tools from Mr. Cameron's wagon and repacked them in ours. Mr. Cameron tethered the horse he'd lent Mr. Butler to the back of his wagon and climbed onto the seat, obviously glad to be driving his own team again.

"That stallion of yours was a bit too spirited for me," he told Papa.

Papa reached up and clasped his hand. "We'll never forget you, Sandy," he said. "You saved our lives." Mr. Cameron didn't answer. He just squeezed Papa's hand and flicked the reins. As he went down the lane, he turned once to wave at us.

Papa and Mr. Butler were ready to leave too, when Goliath came loping out into the yard. Cade slapped his forehead. "What are we going to do with him?" he asked. "You'd better take him, Papa. He's a nuisance in the wagon." Smiling, Papa agreed, and he got a long rope from the wagon and tied it around the dog's neck.

Mr. Butler made a great show of slinging a blanket pack over his shoulder. With a big grin, he said to us, "The Bible. Now your father and I have both the troublemakers." His little joke worked. We were still laughing as the two men disappeared in the forest.

When they were out of sight, we said good-bye to the Mackenzies and began to climb into the wagon. "Where's Sam?" asked Cade, who was counting heads. The words were hardly out of his mouth when Sam came out of the cabin holding Morag's hand. When he saw that we were all watching him, his face turned red as a beet. No one dared tease him though, and right away Cade drew our attention away from him by saying to me, "You make a pretty girl, Ned." I glared at him and tucked my bare feet under me, feeling as silly as could be in Elizabeth's old calico dress.

To make amends for teasing me, Cade said, "Come up here, Ned," and he made a place for me between him and Sam on the wagon seat. "We want to talk to you." Awkwardly I gathered up the skirt of Elizabeth's dress, wondering how on earth she ever managed to run in it.

When I was wedged between them, Cade began to speak very softly. "Sam and I have decided that today we will answer no questions. I'm afraid to trust our luck again. If we're stopped, we'll make a run for it."

Sam couldn't wait to put the plan in action. As soon as we were on the road, he took the rifles and the musket from the floor and began to load them. Mama asked him what he was doing. Before Sam could say anything, Cade replied that we wanted to have the guns ready in case we saw any game. That seemed to satisfy Mama, but she couldn't have been paying much attention. She knew very well that we wouldn't shoot game on the road when we'd soon be in the woods.

One mile, two miles, three miles, four miles, and still we hadn't met anyone. Unlike Sam, Cade and I were beginning to hope that we'd make it to the trail without an encounter. Lulled by the warm morning sun on my back, I was lost in a daydream. Then suddenly Sam poked me in the ribs. Just ahead of us, standing in the middle of the road, were two militiamen. Cade slowed the horses, and Sam and I slipped to the floor and grabbed weapons.

"Yes, sir," Cade called out when one of the men ordered him to stop.

At the sound of his voice, Sam and I leaped to our feet and pointed the guns at the two men. "Place your weapons on the ground and be quick about it," Sam ordered. "Now stand back." Taken by surprise the two men dropped their muskets.

While Cade whipped the horses with the reins, I fired my musket in the air. Startled by the report, the horses plunged forward and broke into a gallop. Behind us a shot rang out. Cade screamed and slumped sideways, clutching his shoulder. In a flash Sam returned the fire.

Driverless and out of control, the horses bolted. I tried to grab the reins, which Cade had dropped, but I couldn't reach them. In desperation I crawled out along the tongue of the wagon and managed to catch one rein and fling it back to Sam. If I didn't get the other one quickly, the wagon would smash. Grasping the mare's harness, I stretched as far as I could along the tongue. Just in time, I retrieved the second rein, tossed it to Sam, and crept back into the wagon. Slowly Sam brought the horses under control.

With Elizabeth's help I dragged Cade into the back of the wagon and put a blanket under his head. Sam had the horses at a gallop again, and the wagon was swaying wildly, but Mama managed to open Cade's blood-soaked shirt.

"Be careful, Mama," Cade screamed when she touched his arm. "I think my shoulder's broken."

Blood was oozing from the wound in his shoulder, but Mama could find no trace of the bullet, and she began to bind up the wound. "Slow down, Sam," she cried. "I have to stop this bleeding."

"No, Sam," groaned Cade between clenched teeth. "Keep the horses at a gallop until you see the fort. Those two militiamen probably had horses hobbled in the woods, and there may be other soldiers nearby. They won't be far behind us."

"Hang on tight then and pray that we don't lose a wheel," Sam shouted, urging the horses on.

Mama was white as a sheet. "Pray that you didn't hit one of the militiamen," she retorted, "or we'll be in even greater trouble."

The thunderous pounding of the hooves and the rumbling of the wagon drowned out her words. To add to the din, the terrified children screamed and screamed, no matter how Elizabeth tried to comfort them. I thought that wild ride must go on forever, but suddenly the walls of Fort Stanwix loomed up ahead of us.

Sam slowed the horses a little, and I leaned over the edge of the wagon searching for the trail, but it was Sam who spotted it first and steered the wagon into its narrow tracks.

"I'm going to have to slow down," he said, "or

the wagon will fall apart on this rough trail."

Mama was looking anxiously at Cade. He was pale and obviously in great pain, but he was conscious and kept urging Sam to keep going. Then all at once we turned a bend in the trail and saw a group of Indians walking towards us.

"What shall we say to them?" I asked Mama. "Should we ask for permission to cross their lands?"

"Yes, of course," Mama answered. "After all, we are trespassing."

The Indians stopped in the middle of the trail, and Sam brought the horses to a halt. He was busy with the reins, Cade was stretched out almost unconscious now, Elizabeth and Mama were doing their best to console the whimpering children. It was up to me, but I was nervous. Although I had often seen Indians at the market shed in Schenectady, I'd never talked to one.

"Do you speak English?" I asked cautiously.

"I do," one of the Oneidas answered gravely, stepping forward. "I am called Lodlihont."

There were five of them altogether — short, stocky men with broad shoulders. Two of them were young, just about my age. They all wore deerskin skirts, leggings, and moccasins, but above the waist they were bare, except for bands on their upper arms and a single feather on each head. Lodlihont had a woollen blanket draped over his shoulder.

"We wish to travel through your lands," I said. "We are on our way to Canada."

Lodlihont didn't reply. He walked to the wagon and peered at Mama and Cade. "Has the boy been shot?" he asked.

Mama nodded and pointed to Cade's shoulder.

"Is the bullet still in his shoulder?" Lodlihont asked.

"No, thank God," Mama replied. "It passed right through, but I think the bone is broken."

"What is your name?" Lodlihont asked.

"I am Martha Seaman and these are my children."

Lodlihont smiled. "Your man awaits you at our camp." He looked into the wagon as though counting us, and I felt his eyes rest on my bare feet. "You are fortunate to have many sons," he said to Mama.

Mama's eyes filled with tears. At that moment she was thinking only of Cade. There was little comfort in Lodlihont's obvious thought that if something happened to Cade, there were others to take his place.

"Who shot your son?" Lodlihont went on, not noticing Mama's tears. "Were there soldiers on the road?"

"Yes," Mama said, pulling herself together. "There were two of them, a few miles east of the fort, but there may be others nearby."

"We shall walk to the road," Lodlihont said. "We'll try to convince the soldiers that you took the road to Oswego. Don't worry, Mistress Seaman. You are safe now."

Mama thanked him shyly, and he raised his hand in a solemn salute. Exhausted after the hard drive, Sam handed me the reins. Urging the horses forward, I began to worry about Cade. Would Mama be able to take care of him in the wilderness?

"I pray you didn't hit one of the militiamen," Mama said to Sam once more. This time he heard her.

"Of course I didn't hit them," Sam blustered. "I was only trying to make them take cover to give us more time."

Through his pain Cade groaned. "Sam is right, Mama. If he hadn't fired, the militiamen might have shot at us a second time and hit one of you."

In a few minutes we came upon a clearing dotted with small bark shelters. Before the wagon had come to a stop, Goliath bounded from one of them, yelping wildly. Papa and Mr. Butler were close behind him, broad smiles on their faces. Their relief quickly changed to alarm when they saw Cade lying in the wagon. Gently they lifted him out and laid him on a blanket on the ground.

There seemed to be only one other person in the camp — an Indian woman, who took one look at Cade and rushed to the fire for an iron kettle of hot water. Mama bathed Cade's wound, and Papa poured a little whisky on it to prevent infection. Cade shrieked

when the fiery stuff touched the open wound, and
Papa gave him a little to drink. Cade turned his head
aside. "It will make me sick," he moaned.

The Indian woman handed Papa some crushed
twigs and nodded at Cade. When Papa just stood
there looking puzzled, she put a twig in her mouth
and began to chew it to make Papa understand that
she wanted him to give Cade some.

All at once I remembered that I was still wearing
Elizabeth's dress and I couldn't get out of it fast
enough. In the wagon I found my breeches and went
to change behind a tree. When I came back, Cade
was quiet. The twigs seemed to have helped him,
though I couldn't understand why.

Papa and Mr. Butler were all for getting away from
the camp as soon as we could, but Mama's "No, Cade
must rest for a while," was very definite. We were still
there when the Oneidas returned two hours later.
Lodlihont told us that they had met six militiamen at
the fort and had persuaded them that we had taken
the road to Oswego, travelling fast.

Mr. Butler gloated. "By the time they discover
they're on a wild-goose chase, we'll be miles into
Oneida territory."

Lodlihont grinned when he noticed me in my
breeches and shirt. "You didn't fool me," he said. "I
knew you were a boy when I first saw you."

That broke the ice, and I plucked up the courage

to ask him about the crushed twigs. "They're willow twigs," he explained. "The juice of their bark drives away pain."

Mama was anxious to talk to Lodlihont too. "Did Sam hit one of the militiamen?" she asked him.

"No," he answered.

"Thank God for that," Mama murmured.

Sam was exasperated. "I've already told you," he said to her, "that I wasn't even trying to hit them."

Papa didn't like his tone of voice and chided him for having fired at all, but Mr. Butler took Sam's part. "You're wrong, Caleb," he said. "It was the only way to gain a little time. Where would we be if the soldiers had seized the wagon? Cade may be wounded, but at least we're all here together."

"Yes, yes," Mama murmured, stroking Cade's hair lovingly.

Chapter Nine

New Friends

"You should stay with us many days until your son's wound is healed," Lodlihont said to Papa. "You will be safe here."

Weak as he was, Cade didn't give Papa a chance to answer. "Thank you, sir," he said, and his voice was surprisingly strong, "but I don't want my family to linger here because of me. Those militiamen won't be put off our trail for long. They'll be back and may even follow us into your lands. The sooner we leave, the better. I can ride in the wagon for a few days."

"My son is right," Papa added. "We must get as far away from the militiamen as we can in a hurry."

Oddly enough, it was Sam who voiced a very practical reason for not leaving at once. "Papa," he said, "I don't think the wagon will hold up unless you do some work on it. That mad dash to reach the trail loosened every bolt in it, and the wheels were getting wobbly too."

Mr. Butler clinched the argument. "Caleb, I think Lodlihont is right. We'll make better time on the trail if we're all well rested, and we should be safe here until tomorrow at least."

I think Papa really wanted to be persuaded, for he nodded his head and said, "Very well. We'll leave in the morning." He and Mr. Butler lifted Cade gently from the blanket and carried him into one of the shelters.

When Papa came out of the shelter, he was all briskness and bustle. Whistling one of his favourite tunes, he crawled under the wagon, where he poked and prodded at the bolts that held the boards together. Then he got to his feet and kicked the wagon wheels. "I'll have to take the wheels off so that I can tighten the rims," he said. "They're loose too."

Papa was his old self again and he began to tease Mama, who was already busy washing clothes at the river's edge. "Well, Mrs. Cameron," he said, "are you glad to have your real husband back?"

Mr. Butler chuckled. "You're lucky that Sandy didn't run off with her, Caleb."

Mama's head snapped up indignantly, a sharp reply on her lips, but when she saw the tender glint in Papa's eye she laughed too. "Away with you both," she said, ducking her head and rubbing very hard at the shirt in her hands.

Suddenly Papa's face was serious. "I knew the day I met her how lucky I was," he said, almost to himself, and he went over to Mama and drew her to her feet. Mama stood for a moment in the circle of his arms, smiling at him lovingly, and for the first time in days my world was bright again.

Soon there were dripping shirts and petticoats hanging from every bush. Papa's tools were spread out around him. Through the camp rang the squeals of the children, playing tag with Elizabeth. We seem to be making very free with the camp of the Oneidas, I thought to myself. I wonder if they mind. But it was clear from the beaming faces all around me that the Oneidas enjoyed having us there.

Mr. Butler's voice broke into my thoughts. "I have a job for you, Ned," he called. "Come and help me gather some of these weeds."

They were green weeds that I didn't recognize and they had a very sharp, unpleasant odour. When we had a small pile of them, we crushed them to a pulp in a big earthenware bowl of Mama's. Then we strained the pulp through a cloth, and an oily liquid oozed out into a pan we'd placed under it. Once the pan was full, Mr. Butler poured the liquid into a jug. All I did was follow orders. I had no idea what we were doing or why we were doing it, and the only thing Mr. Butler would say was, "Horse balm. You'll be glad of it later."

In the meantime Papa had taken some coals from the campfire and started a fire of his own on a flat rock. The Indians, who were friendly and interested, sat in a circle around him watching him work. When Papa had everything set out just as he wanted it, he turned to Lodlihont.

"May we hunt in your lands?" he asked. "We need fresh meat."

"Take all the game you need," Lodlihont answered. "For now there is still plenty, though we fear what tomorrow will bring. Each day the settlers come closer, and soon the game may disappear. When we complain to the governor of New York, he sends agents to talk to us, but they only tell us to raise cattle as the white man does."

"I thought you were raising cattle," Papa said.

"We have some in our large villages," Lodlihom replied, "but the Oneidas are hunters — and venison tastes better to us."

When Sam appeared, Papa told him that we had been given permission to hunt. "Why don't you go into the woods right now and see if you can get us some rabbits or a few pigeons for supper?" Papa added.

Sam's face lit up. He took the rifle from the wagon and whistled for Goliath, who started barking wildly as soon as he saw the firearm.

By now Papa was checking the stallion's shoes to find out whether they were loose. Suddenly some of the Oneidas got to their feet. Two Indians we hadn't seen before were approaching the camp, leading a horse with a pack on his back and a string of trout trailing down his flank. It didn't take Papa long to notice that the horse was favouring one rear foot. When the men greeted him in English, the first thing he said was, "What's wrong with your horse?"

"We're not sure," one of the men replied. "That's why we've come back to camp. Maybe he was scratched by a thorn, or maybe he's picked up a stone."

While they were talking, our stallion began to snort at the strange horse. Papa hastily finished securing a loose shoe and told me to take him away and tether him. As soon as I had the big horse tied up some distance away, I hurried back to the group around the fire.

"I'm a blacksmith," Papa was saying, "and I've had a lot of experience with lame horses. Will you let me take a look at him?"

"Yes, we'll be glad of your help," one of the men replied.

My father tried to coax the lame horse to lift his foot, but the horse didn't know him. Papa had to dodge a few kicks before the Indians got a grip on him and held him still. Then grasping the foot firmly, Papa lifted it and turned it over so that he could see the underside.

"I'm pretty sure there's a stone in there," Papa said, puffing hard.

"We wondered about that," one of the Indians repeated, "but the swelling's on top. Maybe he was scratched by a thorn."

"You may be right," Papa admitted, lowering the foot to the ground and jumping out of the way as the horse aimed another kick at him. "In any case, we have to get rid of that swelling. Will you let me put a poultice on it? If there's a stone in there, it probably got into the soft frog of the foot and worked its way up. The poultice will burst the swelling, and the stone will come out."

The Indians agreed at once that a poultice was a good idea. Papa went to the wagon and began to rummage around, but he couldn't seem to find what he wanted. "Martha, have we used up all the turnips?" he called out to Mama.

"I don't think so," she answered. "Look in the basket under the wagon seat."

Mama wasn't really paying much attention to Papa. She was busy chopping up smartweed. When it was ready, she went into the bark shelter where Cade was resting. I heard a howl of protest from Cade and knew she had put the smartweed on his wound. It was her favourite remedy for cuts, but it was a painful one. The weed was well named.

Papa looked up from the bowl of turnip scrapings he was mashing into a poultice. "Be brave, Cade," he called out. "The smartweed will do you good."

When Papa had warmed the poultice, the two Indians grabbed their horse and held him still, while Papa tied it firmly over the swelling. The horse settled down almost as soon as he felt the heat.

"I'll put a fresh one on tonight," Papa told the men in a satisfied tone, and he picked up his hammer to attack the wagon wheels again.

A sudden shout from Elizabeth caught my attention. It was easy to see that the children were plaguing her, and suddenly I felt guilty. While I'd been wandering around the camp without a care, Elizabeth had been tied to those children. She seemed to spend most of her time with them.

To try to make amends, I started to help her spoon mashed up potatoes into bowls. Then I took Stephen on my lap and fed him. They were good while they ate, even Sarah, but as soon as they had finished, they were off again. We just couldn't get them to lie down for a nap. They were too excited. Finally Papa's temper flared up when Sarah almost fell into the fire. "Take them for a walk," he snapped at Elizabeth and me.

In the middle of the afternoon we heard a great whoop — and Sam appeared in the clearing, brandishing a big turkey. My mouth began to water the moment my eyes lit on it. After I had helped Sam draw and pluck the bird, we took it to Mama. She beamed when Sam handed it to her, almost staggering under its weight. Sam was so pleased with himself that he agreed to look after the children for a while.

That was what Elizabeth and I had been waiting for, a chance to get away by ourselves. It was a hot afternoon and the river was very tempting. Very quietly, so that no one would notice, we stole away from the camp and walked along the bank.

Elizabeth and I loved to swim, but she had to do it secretly so that Mama wouldn't find out. We were certain Mama would frown on swimming as a most improper pastime for girls. If she'd only known, Elizabeth was the best swimmer in the family. She could hold her breath much longer than I could, or even Sam and Cade, and she was like a fish under water.

When we thought we were a safe distance from the camp we took off our clothes and plunged into the river. Cool and refreshing, the water rippled over our itchy skin, soothing our mosquito bites. I could have stayed there for hours, but Elizabeth was always conscious of the fact that she was doing something she shouldn't. Besides, her hair was thick and curly and took forever to dry. If it wasn't dry when we went back, Mama would suspect something at once. The other thing was that we didn't want to leave Sam with the children too long. His patience would soon run out.

Reluctantly, about an hour later, we started back. As we approached the camp, the enticing smell of roasting turkey drifted towards us, lending wings to our feet. The bird was stretched on a spit over the fire that Papa had made. Mama was kneeling beside the fire making scones. Papa was talking to Lodlihont, who wanted us to share their meal. My father was equally determined that the Indians would come to our feast. In the end we all ate together, their food and ours as well.

While we seated ourselves in a circle on the ground, Papa carved the turkey and Mama heaped a pewter plate with scones. In the place of honour in the middle of the circle was a bright red mound of juicy strawberries, which Sam and the children had picked. Smiling broadly, Lodlihont and the Indian woman, whose name was Kahawit, placed a large iron kettle of stew and a wooden platter of golden-brown trout beside the strawberries.

The fish and the scones disappeared quickly, but the Indians didn't seem to think much of our roast turkey. When I peered into their iron kettle, I felt the same way about their stew. There was a muskrat head floating right on top. For a second I felt a little queasy, and Mama looked rather doubtful too, but we both took a little of the unfamiliar fare. The only one of us who really enjoyed it though was Mr. Butler, who kept dipping a wooden ladle into the kettle. Obviously he'd eaten that kind of stew before and liked it.

After supper, while Mama was packing away the leftover turkey, Papa and I went to change the poultice on the lame horse. The animal seemed to trust Papa now. I was able to hold him still while Papa peeled away the turnip scrapings, to reveal a swelling almost twice the size it had been earlier.

"That's about to burst," Papa said. "Ned, can you get my knife out of my pocket?"

By now the Indians had gathered around and they held the horse steady while Papa pricked the skin in the middle of the swelling. Immediately a thick, green fluid gushed from the wound and spilled over the ground.

"Keep a good grip on him," Papa told them, and he pressed the swelling between his thumbs. More of the foul liquid poured out. With a grunt of satisfaction, Papa began to probe the wound. In a moment he held up a tiny chip of stone. "I thought it might take longer," he said, smiling. "The foot will heal quickly now."

For a moment the Indians looked at the chip and then they all began to laugh. As Papa walked away, Lodlihont called out to him, "You are a good medicine man," and Papa chuckled too.

It was a bright starry night, and Sam and I couldn't bear to be cooped up in one of the bark shelters. We spread our blankets on the ground. Soon Papa and Mr. Butler joined us, but Mama made Elizabeth stay in the wagon with Stephen, Smith, and Sarah. She took the baby with her into the shelter where Cade was already asleep.

Two or three times in the night Cade's groans woke us, and we heard Mama soothing him. Once Kahawit went into the shelter with a handful of twigs, and then all was quiet for a few hours. Towards morning Cade cried out sharply. Papa persuaded him to take a few sips of whisky, and after that we all slept for another hour.

In the soft sunshine of the early morning, we repacked the wagon. Mama was just settling her spinning wheel exactly where she wanted it when Kahawit shyly offered her a gift. It was a carved board about a foot wide and two feet long, rounded at the corners, with a small ledge at the bottom. From the sides dangled wide strips of deerskin decorated with bright beads. Neatly folded on top of it was a coloured blanket, and stretched across the end was a leather strap with thongs hanging from it.

Mama was bewildered until Lodlihont explained. "It is a cradle for the baby," he said.

Mama wasn't much wiser, but she smiled and said, "Please thank Kahawit for me and tell her we'll never forget all her kindness."

Shy as she was, Kahawit had to make sure that Mama knew how to use the cradle. She wrapped Robert in the blanket and strapped him to the board. We watched fascinated. When she had secured the board to Mama's back, Robert seemed to be hanging from a strap around Mama's forehead. To our surprise he was cooing quite happily.

Papa made a last check of the wagon, shook Lodlihont's hand, climbed aboard, and murmured a gentle "Giddap." The horses moved on and so did we, all of us on foot except Cade. Mama had insisted that he lie on the floor of the wagon, but before long he began to complain that the jolting was causing more pain than walking would. Papa stopped the wagon, and Cade climbed over the side before anyone could help him. Mama made a sling for his arm so that the weight wouldn't drag at his shoulder.

My feet plodded on and on, one after the other, but my mind was still back at the camp. "I wish we could have stayed there," I said aloud.

Mama knew what I meant. "The Indians were very kind to us and made us feel safe and at home in their camp," she murmured.

Elizabeth laughed. "What about the cradle, Mama? Do you like it? Will you carry Robert all the way to Canada in it?"

"I don't know," Mama answered. "He seems rather cramped. I wonder where Kahawit got it?"

"I imagine she made it during the night," Mr. Butler said. "Before we reach Oswegatchie, you'll be grateful for it."

For the next few miles the going was easy. Even the children were walking without any trouble. But by mid-morning the trail was beginning to rise steeply, and the forest was closing in on us, blocking out the sun.

"We're climbing out of the Mohawk valley," Mr. Butler told me.

His words made home seem farther away than ever. Nothing but unknown wilderness all around us. I wondered how long it would be before we saw another person and what would have happened to us in the meantime.

Chapter Ten

Crossing the Ridge

"Look at that!" Cade exclaimed, as we came out of the forest into a sunlit meadow. Ahead of us was a steep wooded ridge stretching east and west as far as we could see. The thin, grey line of the trail led straight up through the trees.

"Do we have to climb that hill?" Papa gasped in dismay

"I'm afraid so," Mr. Butler replied. "If there were an easier route, the Oneidas would know about it, and their trail would follow It." He stood musing for a moment and then went on very firmly, "Somehow we have to climb the hill, cross the crest, and work our way down the other side. After that we should be all right. The trail goes overland to the foot of a great waterfall the Oneidas call the High Falls."

"How far is that from here?" Papa asked.

"About two days' march on foot — maybe three or four with the wagon. That's the obstacle. We'll never get a loaded wagon up that hill "

Shielding his eyes with his hand, Papa peered up the hillside, his troubled thoughts chasing each other across his face. But he liked a challenge, and finally he nodded, looking determined. "You're right, Truelove," he said, "but I'm sure the horses could manage with an empty wagon. We'll have to carry the cargo, a little at a time."

Suddenly Papa was like a general planning a campaign. "Martha," he said, "you and Cade and the children make yourselves as comfortable as you can here, while the rest of us deal with the first load. After we've made our first climb, we'll have a better idea of what we face."

Papa's determination was contagious. Sam unhitched the horses and hobbled them. Then with a flourish he shouldered the barrel of flour. Not to be outdone by Sam, I slung Mama's spinning wheel on my back, balancing it with my right hand, and stooped to pick up Mr. Butler's jug of horse balm in

my left. Elizabeth, Papa, and Mr. Butler were soon
burdened like pack horses too.

For a while we mounted steadily and at a good
pace, though the going was rough, but then we
began to flag a little. About a mile up the hillside, the
trail levelled off on a small plateau. Mr. Butler told
us to drop our packs and have a short rest, and
nobody argued with him.

"The next climb will be easier," he encouraged
us. "The trail isn't so steep, and I can see a clearing
about two miles up."

Papa was studying the hillside again, obviously
with some new plan in mind. At last he said, "I think
the team could pull a small weight from here. Let's
go back and get the horses and the wagon."

Elizabeth and I were the first to reach the meadow
at the foot of the ridge, and Mama jumped to her feet
when she saw us back so soon. We were in the midst
of explaining the new plan to her when Papa and Mr.
Butler and Sam arrived. Fed up with being treated
like an invalid, Cade said firmly, "I'm coming with
you this time." Mama protested, but Papa convinced
her that Cade wouldn't come to any harm.

We emptied the wagon, and then Papa and Sam
hitched up the horses and set off up the trail. Cade
followed them with a block of wood in his good arm,
ready to drop it behind one of the rear wheels if the
wagon began to slide. Mr. Butler, Elizabeth, and I,

bowed down with as much as we could carry, were not far behind them. This time we left Mama alone with the children. She was telling them a story, and for a change they were quiet.

When we reached the plateau, Papa said to Cade, "That's enough for now. You stay here with the horses. We won't be long.

On our third trip up the trail, Papa was lugging the anvil in his arms, and it was all he could do to hang on to it. Every few minutes he had to stop and set it down. Once I heard him mutter to himself, "I've got to do it. I'd be lost in Canada without the anvil."

Mr. Butler dropped his pack and said to Papa, "Maybe we can tie a rope around it and pull it." Even dragging the anvil was hard enough. There were so many obstacles in the path. Several times we had to steer it around rocks or untangle it from the bushes.

When we reached the plateau, there was no sign of Cade. The stallion was tied to a tree and hobbled, but he was restless and trying to break away. Papa rushed to soothe the big horse. Before he could utter a sound, we found out what the trouble was. Suddenly we were beset by a swarm of small black flies.

I was used to mosquitoes, but I'd never seen anything like these pests. They even penetrated our clothes. Before long blood was trickling from the open wounds they left on my face.

"Where's the horse balm?" Mr. Butler shouted, rummaging among the bundles piled near the wagon. When he found the jug, he told us to cup our hands and began to pour the messy liquid into them.

"Rub it on your hands and faces and necks, even in your hair," he called, rushing towards the stallion. I made a face at Elizabeth, but she was already smearing the balm over her skin, and it seemed to work a miracle. Almost at once the flies stopped swarming around her.

"The wind has dropped," Mr. Butler said as he coated the stallion with balm. "When we came up the hill the first time, it was blowing hard. That's why I didn't notice the flies or think about the horse balm. When it's calm, these pests come in swarms."

The stallion settled down, and Papa and Mr. Butler rushed up the trail, calling Cade's name. Soon I heard Papa scolding gently in the tone he used to soothe the horses. Then he appeared, leading the prancing mare. Right behind him came Mr. Butler, half carrying Cade, whose face was covered with bites. I thought he had fainted, but when Mr. Butler propped him on the ground against a wagon wheel, he managed a wan smile. Elizabeth rushed to apply horse balm to his skin.

"The mare went wild and bolted when the flies attacked her," Cade explained. "I was busy hobbling the stallion and couldn't catch her in time."

"Don't try to talk, Cade," Mr. Butler said. "It's not your fault. I should have hobbled the horses before we went back down the hill."

Poor Cade looked sick, and his face was beginning to swell. "Try to rest, Cade," Papa said. "Ned will stay with you and look after the horses while the rest of us go back for another load. One more trip should do it."

I piled some blankets behind Cade to make him more comfortable, and he dozed off. Then I moved the horses, one by one, for they had eaten all the grass on their small range.

About an hour later the others returned — Sam, Mama, and Papa first, each of them carrying a child and an assortment of bundles. Then Elizabeth appeared, with Robert strapped to her back on the Indian cradle, and a basket of supplies in each hand. Last of all came Mr. Butler, shouldering all the odds and ends.

It was noon now, and we were all as hungry as bears. While Mama and Elizabeth went to look for the leftover turkey, Papa gave the horses some of the precious small hoard of oats. He knew they had a hard afternoon ahead of them.

As soon as we'd eaten, we sorted out the anvil and some of the other things that were awkward to carry and packed them in the wagon. Papa watched us closely to see that we didn't overload it. Then we all fell in behind the wagon, and Papa led the horses up the trail. Sam and Mr. Butler and I were carrying heavy packs, and even Cade had a bundle in his good arm. Elizabeth had Robert on her back and was holding Smith by the hand, while Mama led Sarah and Stephen. She had decided it would be a good idea to wear off some of their energy, and they walked fairly well when they had to.

About mid-afternoon Sam and Mr. Butler and I reached the clearing, just behind Papa and Cade, but there was no time to rest. We had to go back down for one more load. On the way we passed Mama and Elizabeth and the children — much less brisk now than they had been earlier.

An hour later the long haul was finished. I was hoping we could spend the rest of the day in the clearing, but Mr. Butler said no. He pointed down a slope to a sheltered valley with a stream running through it. "That's the place to make camp," he said.

Just before dusk we settled for the night at the edge of the stream. Cade asked me to get him some willow twigs, and I knew his shoulder must be sore. While Mama made us some supper, Elizabeth fed the baby a thin gruel of cornmeal. Mama was so tired that she couldn't nurse him.

Papa watched her with a frown on his face. I knew what he was thinking. Game and fish and berries were plentiful; we wouldn't starve. But we were running out of cornmeal. If Mama couldn't nurse the baby, what would he eat?

We didn't have to be urged to go to bed that night. Mama and Elizabeth took the children to the wagon, and the rest of us spread our blankets near the glowing fire. I ached in every bone, but oddly enough I was happy. Climbing the ridge had been like climbing into another world, and Captain Fonda and the militiamen seemed much too far away to pose any threat.

Just as I was drifting off, a piercing howl brought me bolt upright. Beside me Mr. Butler stirred and sat up too. Goliath began to growl, and Sam pulled him down beside him. Papa got up to throw more wood on the fire. No one had to explain that howl. Wolves were gathering on the ridge.

In a moment Mr. Butler yawned and stretched out again. Papa looked surprised. "Shouldn't we stay on guard for the wolves?" he asked him.

Unconcerned, Mr. Butler rolled himself in his blanket. "No," he replied. "They won't come near us. They're just curious."

"That may be," Mama called from the wagon, "but I wish they'd stop howling. I won't be able to sleep a wink."

And that turned out to be true for all of us except Mr. Butler. Although we were dead tired, we listened for the wolves the whole night through, dozing off now and then, but never for long.

Early in the morning we were on our way again. We thought we'd reached the crest of the ridge the day before, but we were wrong and we had to climb again, a little higher this time. The rough, uneven trail that dipped now and then and climbed again was a constant hazard. Every time the wagon slid forward, we all leaped to hold it back, afraid that it would ram the horses' legs and lame them. Finally Papa and Mr. Butler had to tie ropes to the rear axle so that they could hold the wagon back.

Before coming into the Indian lands, we'd made as much as twenty miles a day. Even the day before we'd probably covered twelve, in spite of all the trips up and down the trail. But that day Papa reckoned that we couldn't have done much more than eight miles.

That night we camped on the crest of the ridge beside the Mohawk River, close to its source where it was only a few feet wide. And the wolves howled again, but we were used to them now. They weren't going to keep us awake.

In the morning we crossed to the east bank of the Mohawk at a shallow ford. I couldn't believe that this was the same broad river that flowed through Schenectady. Just beyond the ford, the trail veered away from the river across the top of the ridge. We were seeing our beloved Mohawk for perhaps the last time.

Soon afterwards we started down the other side of the ridge we'd climbed for two days. The descent proved to be even harder than the climb had been. To get the wagon down at all, we had to empty it again.

Sam and I were leading the horses, always on the alert, so that we could jump out of harm's way if they plunged suddenly. Papa and Mr. Butler were holding the wagon back with ropes again, but when the horses needed to rest that wasn't enough. The men had to prop blocks of wood in front of the wheels. It was slow going.

Mama and Elizabeth soon caught up with us, both carrying packs. Papa watched them for a moment and then he said to Mama, "Martha, much as we need your help, I wish you'd put that load down and go back to Cade and the children. The rest of us can fetch and carry, but only you can nurse the baby."

"I wanted to do my share," Mama answered, "but I know you're right." She dropped her bundle and started back up the hill.

It took us all morning to reach the bottom of the ridge, but once we were down, it seemed our troubles were over. We had descended into a broad valley. In the distance on either side the land rolled gently and the forest loomed.

Not long afterwards we heard Mama and Cade on the trail with the children. Mama settled herself some distance away from us in the shade of an oak tree, where she could nurse the baby in peace. Papa and Elizabeth and Sam went right back up the hill for another load, but Mr. Butler drew me aside.

"I want to show you something," he said. In the soft mud just where the trail led into the meadow there was a track unlike any track I had ever seen before.

"What is it?" I asked.

"A mountain lion," he answered, and I shuddered.

"Cade can't shoot with his bad arm," Mr. Butler went on, "and your father needs me. It's up to you. Get the musket from the wagon and stay on the watch."

Cade saw Mr. Butler loading the musket and came to ask what we were doing. When Mr. Butler told him, Cade frowned. "Ned will never hit a mountain lion with a musket. It's not accurate enough," he said.

"I don't think the lion will come anywhere near the meadow," Mr. Butler answered, "but if he does, a shot will scare him away. Just keep a close eye on the children and don't let them wander away."

"I'll take good care of them," I promised.

When I looked around, I saw Sarah scuttling across the meadow, peering back now and then to find out whether anyone had discovered her escape. I dashed after her and dragged her back to the wagon. The boys were very obedient, but Sarah just wouldn't mind me. As soon as my back was turned, she clambered over the side of the wagon and was off again. Catching her, I slapped her, but she just laughed at me.

"That was nothing but a love pat," Cade scoffed. Pulling Sarah over his knee with his good arm, he spanked her — much harder than I had dared to do. Her screams rang out all over the meadow, but she didn't struggle when Cade put her back in the wagon. For a few minutes she went on sniffling, peeking at us reproachfully through her wet lashes. Her wiles worked on me. All at once I felt like a tyrant and I walked towards the wagon.

"Don't be a simpleton," Cade called out, well aware that I was about to lift her out of the wagon. "We have three of them to look after. What if they all decide to run away at once?"

About two hours later everyone was back in the meadow. We had repacked the wagon and were ready to set out. There'd been no sign of the mountain lion, but Sam, the big hunter, trailed behind the wagon with a rifle and an oddly reluctant Goliath. He seemed to sense that we were being stalked by some creature that was unknown to him. He stayed so close to Sam that he kept tripping him. Finally in exasperation Sam shouted, "Elizabeth, call this dratted cur. He's more trouble than he's worth."

We watched and watched, the whole afternoon, but we never once caught sight of the beast. Towards the end of the day we stopped worrying and even began to joke about him. Sam nicknamed him Gilbert in honour of our other stalker, Captain Gilbert Fonda. We couldn't make up our minds which Gilbert was the greater menace.

By now I was so tired that I could hardly drag one foot after the other. For once Sam was in sympathy with me. "I've worked like an ox," he muttered.

Mr. Butler overheard him. "We won't have to work so hard for the next few days," he said encouragingly. "We're close to the High Falls. From there the trail wanders through a wooded valley with many open meadows."

Towards dusk we caught a faint humming, which grew steadily louder as we advanced. Then through a break in the trees we saw what seemed to be a billowing cloud of steam.

"The High Falls," Mr. Butler announced triumphantly.

It was an awesome sight, tons of water boiling and leaping down a deep gorge. Not far from the foot of the falls, we made camp. Mr. Butler and Papa decided to take turns building up the fire through the night in case the mountain lion was still stalking us, but I was too weary to care about it. Lulled by the rushing waters of the High Falls, I dropped right off to sleep.

Chapter Eleven

Through a Pleasant Valley

For the next three days we travelled north through the valley of the river the Indians called the Kahuago. After the nightmare of crossing the ridge, those days were a gentle dream. The sun shone, it was warm, and the black flies had almost disappeared. Sometimes the trail climbed a little, sometimes it hugged the river bank, but we were always within sight of the clear, sparkling blue of the Kahuago.

Papa and Mr. Butler took turns driving the wagon, once more piled high with all our belongings.

The rest of us, without the burden of packs, dallied along the way, delighting in our freedom to explore the byways of our wilderness. Papa made only one rule: we must stay within shouting distance.

We were going very slowly so that the horses would have a chance to regain their strength. We had no oats left to feed them. For the rest of the journey they would have to exist on grass, and Papa refused to work them hard.

Frequently Sam and I went off into the woods to hunt turkey and rabbits. Since retrieving game was about the one useful thing Goliath could do, we took him with us. I was entrusted with a rifle, but Sam had to reload it for me. I wasn't strong enough to ram the bullet down the barrel. Although I was sorry for Cade, it was exciting to have a chance to hunt with Sam, and I was getting to be a good shot.

Once we bagged a deer. The venison was a great treat after our steady diet of turkey. Mama saved the hide for moccasins. We would soon need them, for our shoes were wearing out fast.

Sam and I rigged up a frame of saplings, and Mama stretched the deerskin over it to dry. The frame was so big that it hung over the sides of the wagon. Whenever we came to a narrow passage on the trail, two of us had to carry it.

Since Cade still couldn't do anything strenuous, he didn't mind looking after the children. Even

Elizabeth had some freedom. Her carefree laughter echoing along the trail rivalled the song of the birds. At home her life had been a dreary round of chores — caring for the children, knitting, mending, and preparing meals. Mama hated keeping Elizabeth tied to her side, but what could she do? With so many of us, it took all the effort the two of them could muster to keep the family clothed and fed. For Elizabeth those three days in the valley were a dream come true, and she made the most of them, wandering the trail in her bare feet, basking in the sunshine, at no one's beck and call.

One morning Elizabeth and I were loitering well behind the wagon. We had told Mama that we were going to pick berries, and we were, but not right away. First we were going to have a swim.

The moment the wagon was out of sight, we stripped and plunged into the river. Just for a few minutes, we'd promised each other, but we lost track of time. In the sparkling river my responsible sister turned into a water nymph. It must have been half an hour later that the nymph surfaced from a dive with a frown on her face. Elizabeth was back.

"We'll have to run to catch up with the wagon," she said anxiously. "Mama will be missing me."

Hoping the sun would dry us in a hurry, we ran up the trail with our clothes in our hands. Just as we rounded a bend, we came upon a mother bear with her two cubs, munching on a berry bush. Without thinking, we turned and rushed back in the direction we had come from. At the foot of a large pine tree, we dropped our clothes and scrambled up the trunk. It was a silly thing to do, but we acted on impulse.

From our perch we couldn't see the bears and we had no way of knowing whether they had gone back into the forest. While we were wondering what to do, we heard a cheerful whistle. Along the trail came Sam with a string of trout over his shoulder. He looked up startled when I called to him.

"What are you doing up there?" he asked.

When I told him about the bears, he roared with laughter. "Bears can climb trees," he scoffed, "especially big ones like that."

While he stood there chuckling, Elizabeth and I inched our way down the trunk with the rough bark scraping our bare skin. Painfully we dragged our clothes over our stinging bodies. Sam went to scout along the trail. "The bears are still there," he said when he came back, "but if we walk along the river bank, we'll be a safe distance from the trail. They probably won't bother us."

In single file we set out, picking our way very softly. As usual Sam was unconcerned. Although we wouldn't admit it, Elizabeth and I were frightened. My heart was beating like a drum. Just as we passed the bears, a twig snapped under foot. The mother bear raised her head and looked straight at us.

We stood frozen to the ground. No use to make a dash for it. The one thing we knew about bears was that they could outrun a man, but we needn't have worried. The bear watched us a moment, then lowered her head and began to eat again.

For a few seconds we were too stunned to move, but then we resumed our silent walk. When we were back on the trail, we really took to our heels and we didn't stop running until we reached the wagon, which was pulled up in a clearing. Breathless, we threw ourselves on the ground.

"What have you been doing?" Mama asked, all unsuspecting.

That was tricky, but Sam rose to the occasion. He told her all about our encounter with the bear, carefully avoiding any mention of swimming. I'd have liked to ask Mama for some of her soothing ointment for my grazed and burning skin, but I couldn't of course. Elizabeth's secret would have come out.

While we were in the valley, we feasted. There was all the game we wanted. The meadows were scarlet with juicy strawberries, and even the blackberries were beginning to ripen. Each night we dropped lines into the river. In the morning there would be several fat trout dangling from them.

Elizabeth and I almost forgot that our journey was really a flight from danger to a land we knew nothing about. In the morning Papa often had to urge us to hurry so that we could be on our way.

"Think of Mr. Butler's wife and children," he said to me one day when I was dawdling. "They don't know where he is. They must be frantic."

One evening when we were seated around the fire, Papa got the Bible from the wagon and read us some passages about the flight of the children of Israel to the Promised Land. As I listened, the journey of the Israelites began to get all mixed up in my head with our own journey. Weren't we on our way to a promised land too?

When Papa came to the part about the manna from heaven Cade interrupted him. "We don't need a miracle to feed us. We've plenty of game and lots of water."

"I could go on travelling this way forever," I burst out. This was the life for me — no school, no regular chores, no set bed time.

"Indeed," Mama said gloomily. "What would we do when winter came?"

Mr. Butler laughed. "Travelling might be easier. Some Loyalist friends of mine came up this trail to Oswegatchie in the dead of winter a few years ago. As I remember, they didn't have as much trouble as we've been having." Then he turned to Papa. "Caleb, does this journey remind you of your days with the regiment?"

Papa looked crestfallen. "Not really," he answered. "I wasn't in the infantry. Mine was a cavalry company, but I never rode with it. Zebe Seaman sent rebel soldiers to seize me in my own stableyard just as I was setting out to join it."

"I didn't realize that you were caught so soon," Mr. Butler murmured. "That was bad luck."

I could see that even now it hurt Papa to remember the ordeal. "I was tied across my horse and led past all my neighbours," he said. "On the way to Fishkill we had to sleep on the ground beside the road. I was so burdened with irons that I couldn't even roll over."

"Well, my life in an infantry regiment wasn't hard," Mr. Butler said. "We made some long marches, but we had wagons to carry our supplies."

"I'm going to join the army when I'm older," Sam announced. "It would be just the life for me."

Mr. Butler's eyebrows rose. "I thought your father was training you to be a blacksmith."

"Yes, he is," Sam replied, "but I hate it."

A wave of pain crossed Papa's face. Sam noticed and went on at once, "I'm sorry, Papa, but there are so many other things I'd rather do. Besides, some day there may be another war and then I won't have any choice."

It was Mama who answered him. "War may seem exciting to you, Sam, but your father and I have been through it and I can tell you it's a hard and bitter business."

Sam looked a little sheepish, but he wouldn't give up. "Mr. Butler," he asked, "why did you make long marches? Didn't you spend most of your time fighting the rebels?"

"Sometimes a battle lasted no more than half a day. What's more, we spent long months in camps in Quebec." Mr. Butler chuckled. "Some of the officers complained that we did more fighting in the taverns of Montreal than on the battlefield. Army life can be very lazy."

"That would suit Sam," Cade interrupted. "The less he has to do, the better he likes it."

Sam ignored him. "How old do I have to be to join the army?" he asked Mr. Butler.

"In my company the oldest man was sixty-two and the youngest twelve."

"Twelve!" Sam gasped. "That's just Ned's age. Can you picture him as a soldier?"

My face grew hot. Sam always managed to rile me. "I could be a soldier if I had to," I snapped.

"Of course you could," Mr. Butler soothed. "The lad I mentioned was only four and a half feet tall." Mr. Butler knew how to pacify me. That was just my height.

Mama had been staring into the flames, lost in thought. Now she said softly, "Who knows what will happen? Just think of how our life has changed in the past few weeks."

"I have been thinking about that," I piped up, "and there's something that puzzles me. You and Papa have always urged us to tell the truth no matter what happens, but while we were travelling to Fort Stanwix we told lies all the time. What made that right, Papa?"

Papa sighed and thought for a while. Then, instead of answering, he began to hum a tune. "Do you remember it, Truelove?" he asked.

No words from Mr. Butler, but suddenly he broke into song.

> If buttercups buzzed
> After the bee,
> If boats were on land,
> Churches at sea ...

"I don't understand," Cade said, looking very puzzled at this reply to my question.

"It's a song called 'The World Turned Upside Down'," Papa said. "We learned it from the British soldiers during the war. I can't think of a better way to answer Ned's question. Sometimes the world is turned upside down and then we can't always behave as we want to. We had to lie to save our lives, and at least our lies didn't hurt anyone."

But I wasn't really listening to Papa. "Sing some more the song," I urged Mr. Butler. That was all he needed.

If ponies rode men,
And if grass ate the corn,
If cats were chased into
Their holes by the mouse,
If the Mamas sold their babies
To gypsies for half a crown,
If summer were spring,
Not the other way round
Then all the world would be
Turned upside down.

"I still think it's a silly song," Cade said. "'Yankee Doodle' is a lot better."

Mr. Butler laughed. "'Yankee Doodle' is pretty silly too, but I will admit it's a better marching song. 'The World Turned Upside Down' is too slow. I could never keep step to it."

Suddenly a strong gust of wind swept across our fireside, and the leaping flames were flat. "There's a storm coming," Papa said, looking up at the dark blue sky.

As he spoke, huge raindrops began to fall. With a blanket over our heads, Elizabeth and I rushed to cover the children, who were asleep in the wagon.

The lightning came closer, flash after flash, followed by great claps of thunder. Then the wind dropped and the heavens opened up. The rain fell like a sheet, soaking us to the skin. Smith and Stephen woke up and began to whimper.

As suddenly as it had come, the storm passed, but our fire was out and we were drenched and shivering. "Maybe I wouldn't like to stay in the woods after all," I murmured to Elizabeth, longing for a roof and warm walls.

Chapter Twelve

Fording the River

Early in the morning of our fourth day in the Kahuago valley, we reached the Long Falls, where the gently meandering river became a boiling cascade, plunging down over steep rock ledges. While Mama and Cade stayed with the children, the rest of us climbed to a peak from which we could see the mighty waterfall in its entire length.

"What a magnificent sight!" Papa said in awe. "It would make a splendid setting for a mill." Then shading his eyes from the morning sun, he peered northward. "But where does the trail go from here?" he went on. "It seems to have disappeared."

"This is where we leave the Kahuago," Mr. Butler replied. "From here it flows west to Lake Ontario, but we keep going northeast. We should find our trail back near the wagon. It leads to the river bank and a ford to the north shore."

Suddenly I realized that Sam hadn't said a word for once. When I turned, I saw him standing on a rock all alone, his eyes lifted to the sky, his arms outstretched. I asked him what he was doing and he winked at me. "I'm trying to part the waters," he said, "but I'm afraid I'm no Moses."

Papa didn't like jokes about the Bible, but even he laughed at that. "We could use a miracle," he muttered, as he started down the hill, scrambling and slipping on the boulders.

Back near the wagon we poked around in the underbrush, searching for the elusive trail. Papa hacked down a few saplings. When they were cleared away, the narrow trail reappeared, barely wide enough for the wagon.

Fortunately it was a very short distance to the ford. Once we reached it, Mr. Butler waded into the water and, picking his way carefully over the rough bottom, set off for the opposite shore. In some places the water came up to his chest. Cade and Sam would be able to manage the crossing easily enough, but

Elizabeth and I were too short to keep our heads above water in the deep spots, and the younger ones would have to be carried.

"The current is fairly strong, Caleb," Mr. Butler reported when he came back. "We'd better stretch a guide rope between the shores so that we'll have something to hang on to."

From the wagon he took a coil of rope and handed one end of it to Papa, who tied it to a sturdy pine tree. As he crossed the river again, Mr. Butler uncoiled the rope, and on the other side he attached his end securely to a rugged oak.

He came right back to us, nodded to Papa, took Stephen in his arms, and waded into the river. Stephen clung to him, terrified but not uttering a sound. Not Sarah though. When Papa picked her up, she squealed and squirmed, trying with all her might to get into the water. Cade followed them so that he could look after the children on the other side. On the next trip, Mr. Butler carried Smith, Sam helped Elizabeth, and Papa guided Mama, who had Robert strapped to her back I stayed on the south shore to take care of the horses.

Papa and Mr. Butler came back at once. Papa bent to remove his shoes, saying to me, "Take yours off too, Ned. Although I wondered what he had in mind, I did as I was told. When Papa lifted his head, he explained to me that the ford was very rough. We

were going to take the horses across upstream, where
the current was weaker and they would able to swim.

Very proud and pleased with myself, I tugged the
mare lead and followed Papa and the stallion along
the river bank. Swimming with a horse was new to
me. I knew it would be tricky, but I'd certainly be
able to lord it over Sam if I pulled it off.

"Take her into the stream as far as you can," Papa
instructed me. "When she starts to swim, grab her tail
— and keep out of range of her hooves. She'll kick."

Getting the mare into the stream was easier said
than done. She was intent on lapping up great
mouthfuls of water. When I tried to pull her, she
began to paw. Papa slapped her rump, and she
plunged forward, pulling the lead out of my hands
and nearly knocking me off my feet. I lunged after
her and grabbed her tail. After that it was easy. When
her feet touched bottom on the other side, I let go of
her tail and swam ashore. On the bank she whinnied
and stamped the ground until Papa brought the
stallion up beside her. Then both horses settled down.

Papa and I led them back downstream to where
the others were waiting. Just as I'd expected, Sam's
nose was out of joint, until Papa told him that he
could help bring the wagon over. While Cade and I
rubbed down the horses and tethered them, Sam and
Papa went back to the other side

Mr. Butler had distributed the load very carefully

over the wagon, with the blankets and clothes on top, where they would be safe from wetting. He was standing holding the Bible, wondering what to do with it. Papa decided it was too precious to risk and carried it across, held high above his head.

Then the three of them secured the load with ropes and removed the wagon wheels. One by one the wheels were floated to the north bank. When everything was ready, Sam tied a rope to the wagon box and crossed the ford, uncoiling the rope behind him. He harnessed the stallion and attached the end of the rope to the horse's harness. "Giddap, giddap," he urged the sturdy beast, and with a heave the stallion started up the river bank. Soon we heard the scraping of the wagon box at the river's edge on the other side. When the box landed in the water, the front end plunged down, soaking half the load.

Step by step, Sam coaxed the labouring stallion up the bank. With each pace forward, the wagon box was drawn farther into the river. At last it was afloat and gliding towards us, but it made a poor boat, laden as it was. Papa and Mr. Butler, one on each side of it, tried to hold it steady, but in the middle of the river, where the current was strongest, it began to swing downstream. Papa lost his footing and disappeared underwater. When he surfaced, the wagon was yards away from him and he had to swim hard to catch it, but the two men soon had it back on course.

Then, just as they were nearing our shore, the wagon box tilted, spilling most of the load. Mama cried out in alarm, and Papa shouted some words that startled me, but he and Mr. Butler managed to right the wagon, and the struggle began again. Sam kept urging the stallion forward, but it seemed an eternity before we heard the welcome scrape on the shore. The job had been done, but Papa stood at the river's edge, groaning. All his precious iron and tools — and Mama's pots — were lying on the bottom, some in fairly deep water, and most of our clothes and blankets were floating on the sparkling surface.

Sam and I plunged into the water, determined to rescue as many of our things as we could. Without thinking, Elizabeth followed us, but in the confusion Mama didn't notice. Her eyes were glued to her precious sewing box, which was drifting downstream. Instinctively, I swam after it. It got perilously close to the waterfall before I caught it. Fighting my way back against the current, I wondered why on earth I'd risked my life for a trinket — but I knew how much it meant to Mama.

When we'd retrieved everything we could see on the surface, Sam and I began to dive for the pots and tools. We managed to rescue several things, but much to Papa's sorrow we found the remains of his last jug of whisky smashed on some rocks. There was no sign of the anvil. By now we'd churned up the bottom so much that we could hardly see down into the water, and Papa told us to rest for a while and let the sand settle.

While Mama and Elizabeth were wringing out the blankets and clothes, Sam and I made a search of the river's edge. We found some turnips in the shallow water, but most of our food was missing, and so were Papa's shoes and mine.

The tall willows that overhung the river bank blocked out the sun. In the deep shade we stood shivering in our wet clothes, too woebegone to move, but Mama was quick to rouse us out of our gloom.

"Ned, scout along the trail to see if you can find a sunnier spot for us," she said to me, and I went willingly, glad to have something to do.

About half a mile beyond the ford, the woods opened into a grassy meadow bright with buttercups. The golden warmth cheered me, and I rushed back to the ford, shouting, "I've found the very spot." Papa and Mr. Butler had just finished replacing the wagon wheels, and we set off at once.

At our new campsite, Elizabeth and I helped Mama spread out the wet clothes and blankets to dry. Sam and Cade had stayed at the ford to catch some fish. Before long they appeared, holding a string of gleaming trout between them. "Can we eat right away, Mama?" I asked. "We're starving."

"I hope you can wait until the fish is cooked," Mama laughed, walking towards the fire Papa had built.

That fine feed of trout finished the job of reviving our spirits. As soon as we had eaten, Elizabeth and I got a basket from the wagon and told Mama that we were going to pick berries. That always seemed to work. What we really planned to do was find the anvil. At the ford the water had cleared and we caught a glimpse of its polished top glinting on the bottom — a little farther out than Sam and I had been diving earlier.

"I'm going in for it," Elizabeth said. With that she pulled off her clothes and plunged underwater. When she surfaced, she was gasping.

"I can't hold my breath long enough to give the anvil a good tug," she said. "Can you fetch some rope without making everybody suspicious?"

I ran back to camp and beckoned Cade. "Elizabeth and I have found the anvil," I said, "but we need some rope and a little time."

"Leave it to me," Cade replied. In a pinch I could always count on him. From the wagon he took a coil of rope, but just as he was handing it to me, Papa noticed.

"What are you going to do with that rope?" he called.

Suddenly Cade groaned and doubled over. It seemed more Sam's kind of trick than Cade's, but it worked. Papa forgot all about the rope and rushed to see what ailed Cade. I grabbed the coil and fled, with Cade's howls pursuing me along the trail.

At the ford Elizabeth was swimming over the spot where the anvil lay. I uncoiled the rope, tied a loop in one end, and tossed it to Elizabeth. She caught it and dived headfirst into the water. She stayed under so long that I was getting worried, but at last her head bobbed up.

"The loop's too small to go around the anvil," she gasped between breaths. I payed out some more rope to her, and she made a bigger loop. Then under she went again, and this time when she reappeared she was smiling broadly.

"The rope's around the anvil," she called, climbing out of the water and hastily drawing her clothes over her dripping body.

At the same moment I heard a stern voice say, "What are you two doing?" Behind me Mr. Butler was staring hard at Elizabeth's drenched hair and clinging clothes.

To draw his attention away from my sister, I stood right in front of him and spoke quickly. "We've got a rope around the anvil. Will you help us pull it out?"

I didn't fool him for a minute, but he winked at Elizabeth and took the rope from me. One mighty tug, and the anvil was clear of the bottom. Another

tug, a long pull, and it was on the bank at our feet —
Papa's much prized anvil.

"I'll take it to your father," Mr. Butler said, setting
off up the trail, dragging the anvil behind him. "You
two are supposed to be picking berries."

"We'd better do it too," I said to Elizabeth.

By the time we'd filled the basket, Elizabeth's hair
was almost dry and we started back. The first thing
we heard when we reached the camp was Mama's
voice demanding crossly, "Where have you two been?
I needed you Elizabeth."

Elizabeth was at a loss, so I quickly took the
overflowing basket from her and handed it to Mama
saying, "Picking berries, Mama. Don't they look
good?" The trick worked, and Mama went off
smiling with the berries in her hands.

Cade and Sam were waiting to pounce on me.
"How did you get the anvil up?" they wanted to
know. "Mr. Butler wouldn't say much about it."

"Elizabeth fixed a loop around it and we dragged
it ashore."

Sam grinned. "I knew you and Elizabeth had a
hand in it, but Mr. Butler didn't give you away. He's
a good sort, isn't he?"

The next day we began to travel overland, away
from the Kahuago River. For about ten miles the
countryside was green and open, and the going was
easy. Then suddenly it changed, and the trail got very

rough. Often we had to hack away bushes and brambles to get the wagon through.

On the second day we came to a hill of bare, pink rock. It wasn't very steep, but it was smooth. Papa was sure the horses would slip trying to pull the wagon up.

Sam and I climbed the hill with Mr. Butler to find out what lay beyond it. We could see the trail leading overland on high ground, but at the foot of the hill there was a river winding its way through the dense forest. We worked our way down to the river's edge and followed it a short distance. We hadn't gone very far when the water began to churn and boil. Just a few yards ahead the river plunged in a waterfall deep into a rock gorge.

"This must be the Oswegatchie," Mr. Butler said, very excited, "but what are we going to do? We can't get the wagon up the hill and we certainly can't get it down that gorge. Let's go back and talk to your father."

When we returned to the wagon, he said to Papa, "I think we've reached the Oswegatchie River, but the trail goes overland away from it. We're going to have to abandon the wagon and the heavy tools."

That was a terrible blow to Papa. So much struggle and so much effort had gone into getting his tools as far as this. He couldn't bear to leave them behind now; they were too valuable to him. At last he said to Mr. Butler, "How far is it to Fort Oswegatchie?"

"About fifty miles," Mr. Butler replied.

Sam, who had been sitting a little to one side whittling a stick, suddenly broke in. "If we could get our things to the river below the falls, we could build a raft and float Papa's tools to Fort Oswegatchie. We could even take the wagon apart and load it on the raft."

To me it sounded like one of Sam's wild schemes, but I could see that Mr. Butler was intrigued. "Settlers have come to Fort Oswegatchie by raft," he said thoughtfully.

Just then there was another interruption, from Mama this time. The talk of rafts seemed to have stirred her memory. "Elizabeth, did I see you swimming when the wagon upset at the ford?" she asked.

"Swimming, Mama?" Elizabeth didn't know what to say.

We were too dumbfounded to come to her rescue, but Mr. Butler stepped into the breach. "Memory plays odd tricks, Martha," he said.

"Perhaps it does, Truelove." Mama's voice was cold. "But now I remember what I saw." She paused for just a moment and then went on in a brisk tone. "Well, good for you, Elizabeth. Perhaps you can teach me to swim in Canada."

Our mouths fell open. Could that be Mama talking? All those plots to keep the secret from her, and here she was taking it all in her stride. Times were changing for the Seamans.

I just had to strike while the iron was hot. "Maybe we should call you Ma in Canada," I said to her.

That was too much for Mama. She drew herself up and addressed me in a haughty tone. "You'll call me Mama, Nehemiah Seaman, in Canada or anywhere else." When Mama used my full name, I knew better than to go on arguing with her.

Chapter Thirteen

Now by Raft

Cade was single-minded. Still lost in Sam's idea, he hadn't even heard Mama and me. "Papa, what do you think about building a raft?" he asked, just as though there had been no interruption.

"I don't see why not," Papa answered. "We have axes and there are plenty of trees, but could we navigate the river?"

"As far as I can remember, this is the only waterfall on the Oswegatchie between here and the St. Lawrence," Mr. Butler assured Papa eagerly.

"There's still the problem of getting our load to the river," Papa went on.

"I've been thinking about that," Cade replied, "and I'm sure we can cut a trail to the foot of the falls. It will be hard work, but we'll manage."

"Of course we can," Sam and I chimed in, thinking about the journey by raft.

We set to work at once, clearing away the underbrush. It took us two days and cost us many aching muscles, but by the second evening, there was a passable trail to the river bank at the foot of the falls. Even Sarah and Smith had helped now and then, carrying away the brush we cut.

Papa didn't talk much during those two days, but he must have been planning all the time he was working so hard. When our trail was completed, he called us together.

"We're going to have to separate again," he said. "There's no path along the river bank for the horses. I'll have to take them overland — up the hill and along the Indian trail." He turned to Mama. "Martha, will you chance the river with the little ones, or will you come with me?"

Mama didn't hesitate. "With you," she answered firmly.

"I'm going to need Cade and Sam and Ned to help me navigate the river," Mr. Butler interrupted, "and probably Elizabeth too. Can you and Martha manage alone with the children?"

"We'll have to," Papa replied.

That was what I'd been longing to hear. From the moment Papa told us that we'd have to separate, I'd had the sinking feeling that Elizabeth and I would be the ones to go overland with him and Mama. Then, when I thought everything had worked out, Mr. Butler upset the apple cart. "Good," he said, "I won't have to worry about the rapids with so many able hands."

"Rapids!" Mama was dismayed. "Caleb, I insist that Elizabeth and Cade come with us. Cade's shoulder isn't strong enough for a rough journey by raft, and it would be too dangerous for Elizabeth."

Cade protested. "My shoulder is fine now, Mama. I've been using it for days, and the more I use it, the better it feels."

"It's high time you knew the whole truth about Elizabeth," Mr. Butler added. "It isn't only that she can swim. She swims like a fish — better than the boys."

Sam laughed. "The only thing she lacks is fins."

"It was Elizabeth who rescued the anvil," Mr. Butler went on. "She'll come to no harm on the raft, I promise you." Mama pressed her lips together, but at last she said, "What do you think, Caleb?"

"Let them go with Truelove," Papa answered after a moment. "He knows much better than we do what help he'll need."

I glanced at Elizabeth. Her thoughts were clearly

mirrored in her smiling face. She loved the children and she didn't begrudge the hours she spent looking after them, but a journey by raft was something beyond her wildest dreams.

It took us two more days to get everything ready. First we made a clearing by the river at the end of our trail. Papa and Mr. Butler cut and stripped some trees. Cade and Sam hitched the horses to the logs and drew them to the clearing. Heaving and tugging, we placed ten logs side by side, with two more across each end, one above and one below. Papa hammered in the few iron nails he'd brought with him, and then we lashed the logs together with ropes. Mr. Butler whittled saplings into poles that we could use for pushing the raft away from rocks

Then came the dreary job of carrying our belongings along the trail we had made. When the wagon was empty, we dismantled it. Papa and Mr. Butler lugged the boards to the clearing. Elizabeth and I followed, rolling the wheels along the trail.

When we were ready to launch the raft, Papa and Mr. Butler levered it with the long poles. The rest of us pushed. Slowly the raft slid into the water. Sam tied it securely to a big tree on the bank, and we loaded it with all the heavy, awkward objects — the anvil, the tools, the iron bars, and the wagon boards and wheels.

The four days we spent at the river's edge were

busy ones for Mama too. From the carefully dried deerskin hide, she fashioned moccasins for Papa and me. Patiently she cut and stitched a blanket until she had created a huge saddle bag.

We all worked so hard that we hadn't time to brood about how sad it would be to watch Mama and Papa set off up the hill without us, but the gloomy moment arrived all too soon.

The saddle bag was slung across the mare's back. On each side was a large pocket, with Stephen's head peeping out of one and Sarah's out of the other. Smith sat astride the mare, and Robert was strapped to Papa's back in the Indian cradle. The stallion was laden with all the things Mama and Papa would need on the journey. Papa was carrying the best rifle, and Mama was leading Goliath on a long rope. He wouldn't be much help as a watchdog for the children, but he could retrieve game for Papa.

None of us said a word as we watched Mama and Papa climb the hill without mishap, but we were all wondering when we would meet again. The moment they were out of sight, Mr. Butler brought us sharply back to earth. "To the raft," he ordered. "We have no time for brooding."

At the river's edge, we climbed aboard, all except Sam, who untied the rope and gave the raft a push out into the river before he leaped after us. Cade took up a position in the stern so that he could steer with one of the wagon boards, and the rest of us settled ourselves around him.

For an hour or so everything went well. The Oswegatchie was so narrow that we could almost reach out and touch its banks. Drifting along in the shade of the overhanging elms, our aching muscles relaxed, each of us lost in his own dream, we hardly noticed our surroundings. Then the sun began to set and we came back to reality with a start. It was going down straight in front of us. Silently we poled the raft to the shore, tied it to a tree, and made camp. Only then did I venture to voice my fears. "Aren't we travelling west, Mr. Butler?" I asked.

"We have been," he admitted, "but these rivers wind around a lot. I may be wrong, but I still think we're on the Oswegatchie. Even if we're not, we're going downstream. Whatever river this is, it's bound to empty into either the St. Lawrence River or Lake Ontario. The worst that can happen is that we may have a longer journey than we expected."

Sam wasn't worried, and even Cade seemed to accept Mr. Butler's assurance that everything would work out. But my happy mood had vanished, and I could sense that Elizabeth was uneasy too.

Soon after we'd set sail the next morning, the raft was carried around a long bend in the river, but the day was dull and there was no sun. We couldn't tell what direction we were going in now.

"I wish we had a compass," Cade said, peering at the grey sky as though willing the sun to come out.

"It wouldn't do us any good," Mr. Butler said. "We're carrying too much iron to get a true reading."

It was a long day and a disappointing one. After we'd made camp, Elizabeth and I slipped along the shore for a swim, but even that didn't cheer us up much. I couldn't understand why Mr. Butler had said he'd need four of us. There wasn't much for us to do.

That night we settled beside the river again. Before we turned in, Cade caught a batch of trout, which he cooked over a small fire. Trout wasn't much of a treat anymore though, and I was beginning to long for a thick slice of bread smothered in creamy butter.

In the morning the river changed abruptly. The water began to churn, and we found ourselves battling a strong current.

"We must be coming to rapids," Mr. Butler said.

Cade and Sam poled the raft to the rocky shore. Elizabeth and I clambered up the bank behind Mr. Butler and followed him along the river's edge. There was no path, and we had to scramble through the underbrush. A short distance from the raft we caught the sound of tumbling water. Soon it grew to a roar, and through the trees we saw another waterfall, dancing wickedly over the rocks, almost taunting us.

The spectacle seemed to dismay Mr. Butler. "Now I know we're not on the Oswegatchie," he said. "There wouldn't be another waterfall." He stood in silence for a moment and then added, "Let's go back to the raft."

Cade was really disheartened when we told him about the waterfall, but not Sam. To him it was just another obstacle to be overcome. "Why don't we take the raft apart?" he said. "We can float the logs over the falls one by one and catch them downstream. We'll be able to put the raft back together again."

Cade responded well to Sam's challenge. "Well, it will be a lot of work," he said, "but I don't see why we can't do it." He sounded just like Papa, and Elizabeth and I took heart.

"The sooner we start, the sooner we'll be on our way again," I said, getting to my feet.

Mr. Butler stood with his hands on his hips, searching our faces, one by one. Then he nodded. "I knew you wouldn't let me down," he said.

The first thing we had to do was get our load to the foot of the falls. Cade and Sam shouldered heavy packs, and Mr. Butler tied a rope around the anvil so that he could drag it. Elizabeth and I tackled the wagon boards and wheels. It was hard going through the rough growth on the river's edge, but halfway down the hill, the brush got thinner, and near the foot of the falls there was an open meadow.

When the raft was cleared, we dismantled it. Sam and Mr. Butler stationed themselves at the foot of the falls with long poles in their hands, ready to manoeuvre the logs to shore as they floated past. Elizabeth and I went to the top of the hill to send the logs down, one by one. Cade picked a spot halfway down the hill. From there he could see both the top and the bottom and shout to us when Sam and Mr. Butler had caught a log and were ready for another.

Luck was on our side. Sam and Mr. Butler recaptured all the logs, undamaged. It took us the rest of the day to reassemble the raft, but we were so pleased with ourselves that we didn't mind the work.

The next morning Mr. Butler woke us at sunrise. Bleary-eyed and still half asleep, we couldn't understand why he was so excited. "Don't you see?" he said, pointing to the rising sun. "We're travelling east again."

For the next two days our journey was everything we had dreamed of. The river was gentle, the sun was hot, and Sam and Cade did what little work there was to be done. Every now and then, when the heat overcame us, Elizabeth and I flopped over the side and let the raft tow us. When we were tired, we clambered back aboard in our dripping clothes and let the sunshine do its work.

On the fifth day the river changed again. In the distance we could see the water foaming and bubbling. Mr. Butler told Cade to steer the raft to the bank, where he hopped ashore and tied it to a tree.

"I'm going to scout along the shore," he said.

"Elizabeth and I will come with you," I called.

"Hurry then," he answered without looking back.

Just as Mr. Butler feared, the churning water turned out to be a long stretch of very rough rapids. Elizabeth and I didn't have the heart to ask him what we were going to do now, but after a while he made a decision. "Cade and Sam and I will shoot the rapids on the raft," he said. "You two can walk along the river bank, but first come back to the raft with me to get the firearms and powder so that they won't get wet."

Carrying the weapons and ammunition, Elizabeth and I had just reached the beginning of the rapids again when the raft shot past us. I was terrified, and not only for Mr. Butler and my brothers. What would happen to my sister and me if they capsized and drowned? Would we be able to find our way out of the woods and reach Fort Oswegatchie?

I needn't have worried. Not far beyond the rapids, we sighted the raft, firmly secured to a tree at the river bank. Sam was standing in the middle of it shouting, "You missed a thrilling ride!" I was so relieved to see them safe that I couldn't even answer.

A few miles past the rapids, we came to what we thought was the mouth of the river. The water seemed to open out into a lake.

"This must be the St. Lawrence," said Mr. Butler, but he didn't sound very convincing.

Standing on the edge of the raft, he scanned the shoreline. There was nothing to be seen but forest and rocks and open water. Frowning, he turned to us. "Just above Fort Oswegatchie there's a low cliff of brown rock on the south shore and rounded pink hills on the north shore. Here it's the other way around."

"Isn't there any current in the St. Lawrence?" Cade asked.

"We've stopped moving."

"Yes, there's a strong current," Mr. Butler answered. "Perhaps we're coming into Lake Ontario." He paused for a moment. "I must confess I don't know where we are."

Elizabeth was close to tears, and I felt like crying too, but once again Sam buoyed us up. "Well, if we keep going northeast," he said, "we're bound to reach the St. Lawrence."

"You're right, Sam. Of course we are," Mr. Butler said.

We all grabbed wagon boards and began to paddle hard. I turned to ask Mr. Butler something and found him looking puzzled again. Almost to himself he muttered, "It can't be Lake Ontario either. It's too small."

"There's a wind coming up behind us," Cade called from the stern. Sam hoisted a blanket on a sapling mast, but the wind was light and we moved very slowly. For two days we travelled along the lake, sometimes paddling and sometimes drifting with our blanket sail. On the third day, while the sail was up, the wind died completely, but much to our surprise we went on drifting.

"There's a current again," Cade shouted.

Very soon the lake began to narrow, and before long we were in a river again. It proved to be a very short stream, twisting northward and flowing into a much larger river. Along the shore the forest grew less dense, and all at once we saw a cabin hidden among the trees.

Cade swiftly poled the raft to the river bank and ran ashore. While he thumped on the cabin door, we all waited breathlessly. Were we really going to see another human being, someone who could tell us where we were? But no one appeared. Then Mr. Butler began to shout. We had almost given up hope of any response when we heard a bellow from the woods, "Allo," and out of the forest came a man, carrying a child.

"Sarah!" Elizabeth shrieked, rushing towards them. "It's Sarah!"

I thought at first Elizabeth had gone mad, but it was Sarah.

Chapter Fourteen

Lost and Found

Sarah stretched out her arms to Elizabeth just as if they'd parted only a few moments earlier. Her hair was tangled, her face was dirty, and she was covered with bites, but she certainly didn't seem frightened. I was the one who was suddenly filled with alarm. What was she doing here with this stranger? Where were Mama and Papa and the boys?

The stranger was speaking to Elizabeth in a language we couldn't understand, but he seemed perfectly friendly. He had a bushy beard and smiling light grey eyes. Straight black hair fell from his red woollen cap to the shoulders of his deerskin jacket, and he moved silently in his soft moccasins.

"Do you speak any English?" Mr. Butler asked him at once. "I'm afraid I don't know much French."

"Little," the man replied. "Je suis Canadien. J'ai trouve la petite dans la foret, il y a deux jours. Maintenant je vais l'emmener au fort."

"Fort Oswegatchie?" Mr. Butler asked eagerly.

"Oui, Oswegatchie," the man replied, and he pointed downstream. "La. Huit milles." He held up his hands and counted off eight fingers.

"Eight miles?" Mr. Butler asked, holding up eight fingers too.

The man nodded, looking at Sarah cuddled in Elizabeth's arms. He understood that Sarah belonged to us and he gave us a big grin when Mr. Butler thanked him for taking care of her.

None of us dared speak of it, but I knew that my brothers and sister shared my dread. Something had happened to Mama and Papa. As he untied the raft, Mr. Butler tried to reassure us. "I'm sure they're all right," he said. "The worst that can have happened is that they're lost. The soldiers at Fort Oswegatchie will soon help us find them."

We wanted to believe Mr. Butler, but I don't think any of us did. Without speaking, we paddled hard, intent on getting to Fort Oswegatchie. Luckily the current was strong and we moved very swiftly, and yet it seemed an age before we sighted a wooden stockade. Then as we got closer a mill came into view, with piles of lumber stacked beside it, and we heard the whining of a saw.

Cade poled us swiftly to the small jetty, and Sam leaped ashore and tied up the raft. We all ran up the path towards the open gate of the stockade. Even in his anxiety Mr. Butler stopped once and pointed proudly, calling to us, "The St. Lawrence." There it flowed, our hard-won goal, wide and blue and welcoming. If only Mama and Papa and the boys had been with us.

At the gate we gasped out our story to the red-coated sentry. He waved us towards the guardroom and the officer on duty. Just as we entered the parade ground, we stopped dead. There were our mare and stallion tethered to stakes. At the same moment we heard joyful shouts. Smith and Stephen were running towards us, with Mama close behind them.

"Sarah," she shrieked as though the rest of us weren't there. Grabbing her little girl from Elizabeth's arms, Mama buried her face in Sarah's hair. When she could speak again, she turned to Cade. "But where is Papa?" she asked him anxiously.

Cade looked stunned. "Isn't he here?"

"No," Mama answered. "He brought us to the fort and left again right away with some of the soldiers to look for Sarah. Where did you find her?"

"A woodsman who has a cabin farther up the river found her two days ago in the forest," Mr. Butler replied. "What happened?"

"Sarah wandered away from our fireside three evenings ago," Mama answered in a broken voice. "Papa was hunting and I was busy with the baby. As soon as my back was turned, she ran off. Smith came to tell me that she'd gone, but by then she'd disappeared. At first I thought she was just playing a trick on me and I called and called, but she didn't come back."

Poor Mama. I knew how she must have felt when I remembered the time that Sarah had tried to run away from Cade and me.

"Papa hunted for her all night," Mama went on. "We were frantic, but in the morning Papa decided that the only thing to do was bring me and the boys to the fort and get some help to search for Sarah."

"How far were you from the fort when Sarah wandered away?" Mr. Butler asked.

"It can't have been very far," Mama answered. "We got here within a few hours."

"Never mind, Martha. All's well now," Mr. Butler said. "I'll go up the trail to find Caleb and the soldiers and tell them that Sarah's safe. Do you want to come with me, Sam?"

When they had gone, Elizabeth spoke for the first

time, looking very puzzled. "Couldn't Goliath find Sarah?" she asked Mama.

Mama didn't answer at once. Then she forced herself to speak. "We lost Goliath on the second day of our journey. Papa thinks he wandered off to look for you and Sam."

Elizabeth didn't utter a sound, but two large tears pushed out from under her lowered eyelids and trickled down her cheeks. Mama handed Sarah to me and put her arms around Elizabeth.

"If only I'd gone with you, Mama," Elizabeth sobbed. "Goliath wouldn't have wandered away if I'd been there."

"I'm sorry, Elizabeth," Mama murmured. "I know how much you'll miss him."

We were still standing there when a soldier came to tell us that there was food for us in the kitchen. "I couldn't eat a thing," I said to Mama out of a tight throat.

"You need something," Mama answered. "Just try." I didn't really have to try after all. In the middle of the kitchen table we found a heaping plate of fragrant brown bread, fresh from the oven. Even Elizabeth managed to choke down a slice.

Mama didn't eat. She held Sarah, kissing her and crooning to her softly. For once Sarah seemed content to be imprisoned by loving arms. When we had finished, Mama took Sarah away to bathe her and change her clothes. Cade was looking after the boys, and I went over to Elizabeth, who was sitting alone, still with tears in her eyes. Somehow I had to get her mind off Goliath.

"Let's explore the fort," I said to her, and reluctantly she followed me outside.

In the parade ground a soldier stopped us. "How did you find the little girl?" he asked. I told him about the woodsman in deerskins.

"That must have been Antoine St. Martin," the soldier replied. "He's a trapper and he has a cabin on the shore of the Indian River just where it meets the Oswegatchie. There's another fellow there too, a trapper called Pierre."

I wasn't interested in trappers just then. "Indian River" had caught my attention. "That must be the river we came down."

"I thought you came down the Oswegatchie on a raft," the soldier replied, looking puzzled.

"We came down a river on a raft all right," I said, "but it wasn't the Oswegatchie."

"That's hard to believe," the soldier exclaimed. "The Oswegatchie is difficult enough to navigate, but the Indian River is even more treacherous. Angels must have been watching over you on that journey."

"Yes, I think they must have been," I answered with a heartfelt sigh. Then I asked him about the fort, and he offered to show us around.

"The fort was built by the French," he told us. "They lost it to the British in 1760, in spite of a valiant stand to defend it."

"How many soldiers are there here now?" I asked him when we'd walked all the way around the stockade.

"It's a small garrison," he replied, "about forty men." That seemed to remind him that he was on duty and he left us at once.

Elizabeth was a little more cheerful now, and we went back to the barracks to wait with Mama. She was with the children in a room the commanding officer, Captain O'Neil, had set aside for her. The afternoon dragged on and on, and still there was no sign of Papa. Then just at dusk we heard the sentry call, "Men approaching." We ran to the gate to see Papa struggling up the path with his arm around Sam's shoulders. Right behind him were six soldiers and, to my surprise, Antoine St. Martin. Mr. Butler brought up the rear.

It was a noisy, joyous reunion, which the soldiers seemed to relish as much as we did. Captain O'Neil appeared and ordered rum for all the men. Then he invited us to dine with him once the children were asleep. "You'll stay too, won't you?" he said to Antoine St. Martin.

As we were walking towards the barracks, Papa spoke to the trapper. "I have no words to thank you," he said. "I thought I had lost my little daughter forever." Antoine St. Martin seemed to understand, for he smiled and patted Papa's arm.

Never before had we dined in such luxury and with such ceremony as we did that evening. With Mama on his arm, Captain O'Neil led the way into the dining room. Papa followed with Elizabeth. Next came Mr. Butler and Antoine St. Martin, chatting affably as though no language barrier existed between them. Cade and Sam and I were at the end of the line, shabby and self-conscious, but doing our best to live up to the occasion.

The table was covered with a snowy linen cloth and laid with gleaming silver and sparkling glass. At either end stood tall candelabra, and I counted sixteen candles all aglow. Captain O'Neil sat at the head, with Mama on his right and Papa on his left. The rest of us were spread around the big table. A soldier served us, and Cade and I, and even Sam, sat in awkward silence, sipping the wine he had poured for us. The food was good, but the conversation was even better.

"Mistress Seaman told me about Captain Fonda," Captain O'Neil said to Papa. "A most unpleasant rogue."

"Do you know him, Captain?" Papa asked.

"Fortunately, only by reputation," the Captain replied, "but I was intrigued to learn that you had a hand in his capture during the war."

Papa didn't say anything, but it was easy to see that he was enjoying the attention of the elegantly dressed officer.

Then Captain O'Neil changed the subject. "I suppose you are eager to cross to Johnstown as soon as possible."

"Indeed we are," Mama replied. "We're very anxious to be settled."

"There's no boat here just now," the Captain went on. "We're expecting a brigade of bateaux from Kingston, but that may not be for another week. Antoine has a boat though. Perhaps you can strike a bargain with him."

"I have very little money," Papa replied.

Captain O'Neil had a conversation in French with the trapper and then he turned to Papa again. "Antoine will take you across in return for your wagon," he said. "I can't imagine why he wants it; he hasn't any horses. Still, that's his bargain."

"A bargain I accept gladly," Papa replied, smiling at Antoine St. Martin. "Tell him that I'll put the wagon back together for him in the morning. That leaves me with only one problem — how to get the horses across the river."

Captain O'Neil smiled at Mama as though they shared a secret and then he spoke to Papa. "It was dark when you arrived, so you didn't see your horses, but you'll find that they're looking much fresher. My men have been feeding them oats for the past few days. I'm sure they're strong enough now to swim behind the boat."

"I don't know how to thank you," Papa replied.

It was late when we rose from the table, and the wine had made us all very sleepy. We went straight to bed — in quarters that were barren enough, though they seemed luxurious to us after weeks of sleeping on the ground.

In the soft sunshine of the early morning, we all trooped down to the shore, eager and excited about the final step of our journey. Papa and Mr. Butler were already there, busy reassembling the wagon. Before long Antoine St. Martin rowed up to the jetty.

"He must have walked back to his cabin to get his boat while we slept," I said to Sam. Then I noticed Mama. She was gazing doubtfully at the trapper's craft. It was something like the boats on the Mohawk — but a miniature version — a small, flat-bottomed boat with a shaky mast. As far as I could see, there was only one pair of oars, and I began to wonder whether we wouldn't be safer on our raft.

Papa obviously had the same doubts. He came over to the jetty, shaking his head. "It's too small," he said to Antoine St. Martin, pointing to all our belongings piled on the shore.

Almost at the same moment we heard a shout. Coming down the Oswegatchie was a huge bark canoe, responding swiftly to the rhythmic strokes of a powerful man in deerskins, to whom Antoine shouted, "Allo, Pierre."

Now Papa looked even less confident, and he expressed his doubts to Captain O'Neil, who had joined us at the jetty. "Those boats won't hold all of us and our belongings too. Besides, they don't look safe."

Captain O'Neil wasn't in the least perturbed. "The canoe will hold a lot more than you think," he said, "and both craft are perfectly safe as long as there isn't a strong wind." Papa had to be satisfied with that.

My father and I stood silently for a moment, gazing in wonder at the St. Lawrence. The river was calm, with a ghostly mist rising from its surface. "Well, Ned, we made it, didn't we?" Papa said. "If we can live out our lives in peace beside this great river, I'll be content." Suddenly he shook his shoulders and got back to the present. "To work," he said.

It didn't take us long to pack the boats. Then Sam and I began to argue about where we would ride. Papa settled that question in a hurry. "Cade, Sam, and Elizabeth, into the canoe," he said. That was just what Sam wanted. He was hoping that Pierre would let him paddle.

In Antoine St. Martin's boat, Mr. Butler and I settled ourselves in the stern, each of us holding one of the horses' leads. Papa was helping man the oars.

In the bow, Mama, with Robert in her arms, was surrounded by the chattering children.

It was an exciting moment. Papa called his last thanks to Captain O'Neil, while what seemed like all the soldiers of the garrison waved and cheered.

The first pull of the powerful current filled me with awe. We had always thought of ourselves as river folk, for we'd spent most of our lives beside the Mohawk, but it was just a stream compared to the mighty St. Lawrence.

Chapter Fifteen

All's Well

"There it is — Canada!" Cade shouted, pointing triumphantly to the north shore. Then in great excitement we all began to shout, "Canada," all but Papa. His confidence and eagerness of the early morning seemed to have deserted him.

"What's the matter, Papa?" I asked him.

"For weeks I've thought of nothing but reaching this haven, but what are we going to do now?" he answered, "We're penniless in a new country."

Mr. Butler refused to let him be downcast. "Since

you enlisted in a Loyalist regiment, you're entitled to a grant of land, free of all charges. That's a good beginning."

"What do I know about farming?" Papa muttered. "I've been a blacksmith all my life."

"You have three strong sons to help you clear the land and plant crops," Mr. Butler replied in a bracing tone. "Your neighbours will help you too, and you may be able to draw rations from the military stores for a while. By next year you should be able to feed yourselves. All the settlers grow their own food, enough to last them through the winter."

"I thought I might be able to trade my services for food," Papa said.

"Not yet," Mr. Butler replied, "except for a little grain perhaps. Most families are able to grow only enough for their own needs. It takes time to clear the land."

"So be it," Papa answered, determined and more cheerful again. "I'll claim my grant of land, but as soon as ever I can I'll go back to working as a blacksmith."

"You needn't worry," Mr. Butler said, "not with children as resourceful as yours. You should have seen them on the raft; nothing daunted them. They'll make fine pioneers."

Papa smiled proudly. "You're right," he said. "We can do it together."

Suddenly Mama spoke. "Is that Johnstown?"

"I know it doesn't look like much yet, Martha," Mr. Butler reassured her, "but I'm sure you'll be happy here."

On the shore we could see a jetty with a large, open boat moored to it. Behind the jetty were several cabins, almost hidden in the trees. All around the forest loomed, and I wondered if the sun ever penetrated it. But if the forest was gloomy, our welcome was not. The moment our boats touched the shore, people came running from the cabins to greet us.

On the big boat moored to the jetty I noticed a stout, fair man, who was staring at Papa. Suddenly his face broke into a broad smile. "Caleb Seaman!" he shouted, leaping over the side of the boat and striding towards my father.

Papa was thunderstruck, but almost at once he grinned and held out his hand. "Captain Meyers. I'm surprised that you recognize me after all these years."

"You haven't changed much," the fair man answered, "a few more grey hairs perhaps. What brings you to Canada now?"

"Our old friend Captain Fonda," Papa replied, making a sour face.

"Aha," Captain Meyers answered, "seeking revenge, I'll wager. Tell me about it."

Watching the reunion, I couldn't believe that this jolly man was the mysterious spy of long ago, but I liked him at once. He seemed to lift Papa's spirits.

Slapping Mr. Butler on the back, Captain Meyers said, "You were optimistic to risk going into New York, Truelove. I'm glad to see you back safe and sound." Then he turned to Mama. "Welcome, Mistress Seaman," he said. "We've never met, but I used to admire you from a distance when I hid in your loft in Schenectady."

Mama smiled and held out her hand to him. Captain Meyers went on, "Which is the bold son who was arrested with you, Caleb?"

Papa introduced us all. Captain Meyers laughed when he shook my hand. "You're a bit young to attack a militiaman, aren't you?" he asked.

My ears grew hot and I couldn't think of anything to say. That day in the Schenectady jail seemed so far away and so long ago.

Suddenly Captain Meyers grew serious, and all at once I caught a glimpse of the daring spy of years gone by. He almost seemed to grow taller.

"What can we do for you?" he asked Papa. "Where do you plan to settle?"

It was Mama who replied. "As close to Johnstown as possible."

"You'd like the settlement where I live," Captain Meyers told her, "and I could take you there." He pointed to the boat tied up at the jetty. "It's mine. I still farm but I do a little transport business now too. We're on our way home from Montreal with a cargo of rum, but there's plenty of room for you."

"Where is your settlement?" Papa asked.

"About a hundred miles west on the Bay of Quinte."

"No," Mama interrupted, "it's too far away." She was speaking as much for Papa's benefit as for the Captain's. "We've been journeying for weeks. It's a miracle that we've got this far."

My father and Captain Meyers looked at Mama as though wondering how best to persuade her. Suddenly a man standing at the end of the jetty, who had been listening to the conversation, pointed to Papa's anvil. "Are you a blacksmith?" he asked.

"Indeed I am," Papa answered.

The man held out his hand to Papa. "I'm William Clow," he said, "and I can tell you that a blacksmith would be welcome at Coleman's Corners. It's only eighteen miles from here. There's a mill at the village, and it will soon be an important town."

Before Papa could say anything, Mr. Clow went on, "I'm on my way there now and I know I can find accommodation for you and your family among my friends."

"That's good advice, Caleb," Captain Meyers said. "If Mistress Seaman is determined to settle nearby, Coleman's Corners should suit you very well. I can take you as far as the landing at Buell's Bay, about fifteen miles upstream. Coleman's Corners is only three miles inland from there."

"What do you think, Martha?" Papa asked.

"Yes, Caleb, let us go to Coleman's Corners." It was easy to see that the prospect pleased Mama. Before nightfall our long journey would be over.

With a nod of his head, Papa made the fateful decision "What about the horses?" he asked Mr. Clow. "Is there a trail to Coleman's Corners? Could the boys ride the horses there?"

"Horses!" Mr. Clow exclaimed, and Papa pointed along the shore to where Cade and Sam were rubbing down the mare and the stallion.

Without another word, Mr. Clow ran over to them, shouting back to Papa as he neared the horses, "A stallion, no less. Truly, Mr. Seaman, you're a godsend. Up to now we've had no stallion within twenty miles of Coleman's Corners and have been unable to breed our mares." He stared at the big horse admiring him and then went on, "Yes, there's a trail to Coleman's Corners. The boys can come with me."

For a moment Papa was overwhelmed. Everything was working out so well; he'd be able to work at his trade after all. Then suddenly he remembered Mr. Butler. "What about you, Truelove?" he asked. "Where do you go from here?"

"My farm is a short distance upriver," Mr. Butler answered. "Captain Meyers says that he'll take me as far as my landing."

Mama looked at him with a soft smile on her face. "I'm so glad we're settling close to you, Truelove," she said. "It makes me feel at home already to know that you and your family will be nearby."

Mr. Butler clasped Mama's hand. "That's right, Martha. You haven't seen the last of me," he said.

All at once Captain Meyers became very brisk and businesslike. "Let's get this load aboard," he said, kicking at our pile of belongings. "My son Jacob will give us a hand." He called to a blond boy about Sam's age, who ran down the gangplank towards us. Close behind came a big black and white dog, with three fat puppies tumbling after her. They sniffed at each of us in turn, and then one of them settled on Elizabeth's foot, his trusting brown eyes turned up to her appealingly. Elizabeth couldn't resist him. Bending, she picked him up and cuddled him in her arms. We could see the tears in her eyes.

Captain Meyers watched her for a moment, and then I saw him murmur to Mama. She must have told him about Goliath, for he called out to his son, "Jacob, can you spare that pup for Elizabeth?"

Jacob laughed. "Yes, I can, Pa, not that my permission matters. He's already adopted her."

Elizabeth lifted a glowing face from the soft fur. "I'll call him Samson," she said. What a name for that little bundle. Oh well, I thought, he's as much like Samson as Goliath was like his namesake.

As we pulled away from the jetty, the last shred of doubt and fear evaporated. We had come full circle. Barely visible in the distance, Cade and Sam were following Mr. Clow along the trail. Beside me a radiant Elizabeth cradled her new pup. In front of me Mama sat surrounded by the children, all laughing and talking. In the bow, with Captain Meyers and Mr. Butler, Papa stood erect and strong, ready to make a new life for us in this new homeland we'd sometimes thought we'd never reach in those long, hard weeks on the trail.

Jacob came to squat beside me, our escape very much on his mind. "Do you know," he said, "that when I was in Oswego a few weeks ago, delivering supplies to the fort, the soldiers were talking about a man named Captain Fonda. He was in pursuit of a Loyalist family on their way to Canada. Little did I dream I'd meet that family."

That really tickled me. Imagine Captain Fonda combing the road to Oswego while we made our escape on the Indian trail. "The next time you're in Oswego be sure to give the soldiers a message for Captain Fonda," I said to Jacob. "If he wants Caleb Seaman, he'll have to come to Canada to get him."